Phantom Sounds

Stories by
Lyle Roebuck

ISBN: 978-1-945917-32-5
Printed in the United States of America

All characters in this book are fictitious.
All locations in this book are fictitious or used fictitiously.

Cover Image: *The Gossip Fox*, a graffito, *Via dell'Anguillara*, Florence, Italy

Some of the stories in *Phantom Sounds* have appeared previously:

"A Ring of Fire"—*Hoosier Lit*
"The War at Home"—*Straylight Magazine*
"The Crab"—*Phantom Drift*
"A Prayer of Humble Access"—*The Timberline Review*
"Hard Time"—*Wraparound South*
"That Old-Time Religion"—*Redivider*
"*Voyageurs*"—*Arlington Literary Journal*

BIG TABLE Publishing

"Making other books jealous since 2004"

Big Table Publishing Company
Boston, MA
www.bigtablepublishing.com

Acknowledgements

I am grateful to Drs. Robert Lenet, David Kaiser, and Anna Choub. To my friends Andrew and Erin, many thanks. I am indebted to Peter Field and the other editors of the journals in which several of these stories first appeared. Deepest thanks to my editor, Steph VanderMeulen, and to the editorial team at Big Table Publishing Company—particularly Robin Stratton.

"I have the nightmares and I know about the ones other people have."

~ Ernest Hemingway
The Paris Review, "The Art of Fiction" No. 21

Table of Contents

for Wade

Part One

The Executioners of Old

I

MICHAEL'S APPROACH to self-preservation was to sanitize his existence and make a fresh start, most recently with his laptop. He bought a new one, a space-gray MacBook, on which he would keep only documents, music files, and pictures he wouldn't mind showing his mother. From his old machine, he scrubbed all.

It was one month after Easter, and Michael sat nine stories high in the open window of his empty two-room apartment on West Chicago Avenue. The north branch of the Chicago River meandered, greenish-gray, a block east, and when he leaned from the window Michael could see where it passed beneath the twin leafs of a century-old bascule bridge.

As he scrolled in search of a desktop image for the MacBook, he periodically glanced up through the room, windowless except for the one in which he sat. In the absence of furnishings, and since he had only recently moved back to the city, it was difficult for him to think of the place as his. He remembered what his friend, Peter, had said once when Michael was first selling and then giving away his possessions. A Ph.D. student in psychology, Peter was always keen to nudge.

"You seem to be getting rid of a lot these days," he said. "What's that about?"

"Can't I be bored with my things?" Michael said. He had not yet told Peter he was going to live in Europe for a year, and perhaps longer, to disentangle. What he imagined Peter had meant was, "Are you planning to kill yourself?"

It was what the psychiatrists wanted to know when Michael had woken up in the ICU, except when they asked they had used the word "hurt." "Were you planning to hurt yourself?" Michael told them no, which was the truth. But he had taken a lot of drugs. They wanted to know if he had tried to kill himself because, as several people were aware, including Peter, Michael had been in the middle of a rough patch.

Noah, the young man with whom he had been involved, had tried to get Michael fired, just as he had threatened. He had written an email half as full of truths as misspellings, which in their own way seemed to belie Noah's innocence, and he had sent the email to the dean of the college where Michael taught. Not that Noah was a student there. Not that Noah was ever a student of Michael's. And not that it mattered. On the morning Michael was called into the dean's office, the only other person there was the head of human resources, who sat stone-still, a reluctant witness to the fall of a colleague.

Noah had signed his full name to the email, which included a list of allegations so serious the dean wondered aloud why this person had not gone directly to the police. Michael knew why.

Noah had his own troubles. He had twice been arrested for shoplifting and had missed court dates—and those were the things of which Michael was aware. Noah hadn't gone to the police, which was no guarantee he wouldn't at some point. He would *threaten* to, as he had before, but threats are free. He had had little hesitation, however, when it came to hurting Michael where he knew he could: his reputation and career.

"Are these things true?" the dean asked, handing him a printout of the email.

Already aware of what it said, Michael barely skimmed it. Noah had sent him a draft the previous night—taunting him, mocking him, and giving him "one last chance" to save himself.

14

But Michael had only checked his email that morning, an hour before he was called in. "No," he said.

"None of them?"

"None of them," Michael said. He could already feel fate's gravity dragging him down. "Should I talk to a lawyer?"

"I can't tell you not to talk to a lawyer," the dean said.

Upon leaving the office, Michael's first cogent thought was of how his life in the classroom was over. Notwithstanding the prospect of absolution, he could not unwrite what Noah had written. And now there was a record, an email that had been printed and was destined to be copied, filed, and forever preserved. Michael recalled the time he had sat on a jury. It was for a case so dull he found himself paying attention only to the things the judge explicitly told the jurors to disregard. His own was not a dull case. *You will disregard the allegation that Michael Jensen had sex with someone twenty-seven years younger and six months shy of their state's age of consent. You will disregard the allegation of drug use. You will disregard the allegation of sick days taken to engage in said drug use.*

The college conducted a six-week internal investigation, at the end of which the determination was made that Michael's contract for the coming year could be honored.

"We would have no problem having him back," the dean informed Michael through his lawyer, "if he'll sit for the investigators' interview as the others have." With Michael's attorney present, the others had included Noah himself. Noah, who had recently become interested in astrology and was keener to read the investigators' star charts than answer their questions. By the end of the session he had walked back the lesser allegations and made it clear his grievances had subsided such that he had no plans to pursue the matter.

15

Noah's mother, who had known of the romance, was also interviewed. It was not what the investigators were expecting when she told them that, after meeting Michael, she had consented to Noah living with him; that she had thrown him a party for his forty-fourth birthday; that Michael and her husband, James, had gone to Bears games together and shot handguns at the range. Michael's attorney told him of these things. He pressed, "All you have to do is to sit for the interview. You don't have to say much. And I'll be there, of course."

"Did they feel foolish?" Michael asked. "The investigators?" He wanted to hear they had. He wanted to hear they had been stunned by a legitimacy they hadn't expected—by Noah's mother's advocacy for him over her son and by things Michael was sure they had never seen before.

"I doubt there's much they haven't seen," the lawyer said, "and I don't know how they felt, but do you want to keep your job or don't you?"

"I don't," Michael said.

II

Looking east toward Lake Michigan, Michael could see his former apartment building in the distance. It was a place he loved more than the career he had left and far more than he had loved Noah. His apartment there was a loft within what had been, in the previous century, a Victorian-Gothic mansion. There was a Starbucks on the ground level, and the rent was affordable for such a nice neighborhood. It was the apartment in which he and Noah had lived for a year before things went to hell. It was also the apartment, six months after Michael was fired for non-compliance, in which he had overdosed and nearly lost his life.

That was two and a half years ago. And the overdose . . . that had been the real reboot. Michael's heart stopped three times before they got him to the emergency room, where his PSI was six. "Ninety-five is normal," one of the nurses told him the day after he woke from a week-long coma. "Most corpses have more oxygen in their blood when they arrive at the morgue than you did when the EMTs got you here." Michael kept waiting for one of the doctors to tell him how lucky he was, and to say it as a kind of scold. But that didn't happen. As with the investigators, he concluded, there probably wasn't much they hadn't seen.

Michael *had* been lucky, and he was grateful for the luck. Generally unencumbered by the hauntings of religion before the overdose, he was utterly encumbered after.

"Did you see anything?" asked one of the baristas at the downstairs Starbucks. "A light?" It no longer surprised Michael when they knew his business. They had known about Noah, after all, and had gossiped to high heaven about it. The barista was a religious-studies major at the nearby Moody Bible Institute. It was a brave question, Michael acknowledged, and one deserving of a brave answer.

"No," Michael said.

"Something like that happened to my cousin," said the barista, looking less disappointed than Michael had anticipated. "He said the same."

Michael's recovery was speedy. He left the hospital with his mind fully intact, which was more than his family and friends had been encouraged to hope for. Within weeks, he recovered his physical strength and decided that the only thing better would be to build on it. With the time, money, and will to do so, he joined a gym and hired a trainer. Michael saw the next phase of his life begin to roll out, less dreadful than inviting, and he embraced it with a renewed sense of ownership.

Besides being free from feelings of obligation (he always cringed when others who had cheated death talked of the work God had planned for them), Michael was burdened by practically nothing, not least of all a job he had not loved. And if he didn't have a job with its repetitive stresses, frustrations, and disappointments, what did he have? He had money. He had an apartment he loved in a city he loved, and most of all he had time. That commodity others measured by hours in a day he now measured by years in a life—and one still retaining some semblance of its youth, with a body, mind, and spirit not fully set on the inevitable death slope.

Soon after Michael had gotten home from the hospital, Peter visited. Peter was the second person he had called to tell of Noah's email. Noah's mother had been the first.

"They put me on Lexapro," Michael said, sitting forward in his chair. "Now, seriously, do I seem depressed?"

"No," Peter said.

"Good. Because I'm not. And unless it's like cancer . . . unless it's something you can have without knowing it, I don't see why I need Lexapro."

"Are you angry?" Peter asked.

"Who should I be angry at?" Michael said. "Noah didn't make me overdose."

"I didn't mention Noah."

"I don't think I'm angry."

"You know what they say," Peter continued. "Living well is the best revenge."

Michael had heard this, but when Peter said it he breathed new life into the idea. It was as if the concept had been conceived for his benefit alone. What's more, Noah had made such a revenge easy. He had set the table in doing for Michael what he would not have done for himself, shaking him loose from a job he tolerated well enough to have remained stuck in it for the rest of his life. In addition, Noah had recently moved to California, ceding, it seemed, Chicago and the Midwest to him.

For months, things went well. Michael continued to get fit. He looked and felt better than he had in years. He redecorated his apartment. He volunteered. Then, one night in August, his phone rang at four a.m. with a number from an unfamiliar area code. When he answered, it was Noah. Drunk or not, he was demanding money. Calling from L.A. and desperate, he screamed threats, punctuated more than once by the refrain, "I was only a child!"

Michael hung up, blocked the number, and remained awake for the rest of the night. He calculated Noah's age now. Nineteen. Still a child, some would say. He was less alarmed by threats than by the fact Noah had contacted him at all, now more than two years since they had last seen each other. It came as terrible confirmation of what he feared most: how anything that would ever go badly for Noah would ultimately be Michael's fault and how anything that would go well for Noah would do so in spite of having known Michael.

After he had decided to move to Europe, but before he left, Noah made contact again, this time on social media, where he posted a series of insulting comments to Michael's Instagram photos—pokes with a dull stick about his high forehead and fondness for deserts. Michael blocked him. If Noah could yield the Midwest to him, then he, in the spirit of his renewal, would yield all of North America to Noah. Let him grow old in L.A., Michael schemed, where twenty-five is long in the tooth, while he would stroll through middle age surrounded by centuries-old buildings and beautiful art—himself an infant by comparison.

For thirteen months Michael leased a furnished apartment in Madrid, Spain. With modern appointments, the flat was on the fourth and topmost floor of a building that, although refurbished, retained its ancient character. It was near the city center, close to museums and a beach. During this time, Michael traveled out, though never far, to places like Avila, Buitrago del Lozoya, and Rascafría. Enchanted by the blithe simplicity of these places, Michael often fanaticized about relocating to such a town, where English is hardly spoken and he could get by on the Spanish he already knew.

Occasionally, on the crest of a merlot bender, he would surf the web and indulge fantasies of moving to a volcanic atoll like Maupiti, a four-square-mile ring of beach in the Society Islands of French Polynesia, where there wasn't even the internet. He would vanish unceremoniously. He would quit the Western Hemisphere in favor of a place where one US dollar trades for one hundred French Pacific francs and where the export economy is coffee beans, vanilla, and rare black pearls.

In Madrid, Michael spent his evenings reading at outdoor cafés or, when he stayed in, watching movies or science documentaries. So much had changed since high school and his days of undergraduate astronomy. Pluto had lost status, gravitons were a thing, and the universe, with all its spectacular perils, was expanding far faster than previously thought. Yet nothing fascinated him more than the business of quantum entanglement—two particles in different places behaving with unerring predictability. A perfect sameness. Bound by an action Einstein had called "spooky," neither time nor distance takes account of such connections. The astrophysicists in the documentaries called it "non-locality." As he watched, a glass of tempranillo in one hand and fistful of chips in the other, Michael could think of it only as voodoo magic on a subatomic scale.

III

Michael slid from the windowsill into his vacant room. He put his MacBook on the floor and decided to take a walk along the river. In Madrid, he had sometimes gone for walks to stay fit, in lieu of joining a gym, yet it hadn't entirely worked and he had gained weight back. Other than Peter, who had flown over immediately after finishing his doctorate, he'd had no guests during the thirteen months abroad. When Peter arrived, Michael was as ready for a visitor as his friend was for a vacation.

"I can't believe you have this place to yourself," Peter said, "and you haven't had anyone else come stay?"

"Whom might I have had?" Michael asked, wondering if Peter would mention Noah. If Peter wasn't going to bring him up, then he wasn't. And it was just as well. It didn't matter that Michael had known Peter for as long as Noah had been alive, such conversations always seemed to have the underpinnings of therapy sessions, and it would only feel more like that now since Peter had the extra letters behind his name.

"How did you decide to move back to Chicago?"

"Flipped a coin," Michael said.

"Really?"

"I was going to. Then I asked myself which result would least tempt a re-do."

"So, you didn't flip a coin?" Peter asked.

"Didn't have to."

"That's almost brilliant," Peter said.

And like the non-binding flip of a coin, it didn't matter. Michael could sit at home or go for walks just as well in a city he knew as on a rock in the middle of the Pacific or, for that matter, anywhere in between. It wouldn't stop him from wondering about Noah, nor would it stop Noah from contacting him, one way or another, as he had yet again.

While Michael was in Madrid, Noah had gotten hold of his email address and sent a message asking how he was doing. No threats, only a singular nicety. A line, in search of a nibble, cast halfway across the globe. That was when Michael first felt the stir of prophetic wisdom to anticipate the day Noah would reach out to ask for his forgiveness—like the executioners of old.

And so, at forty-nine, he would start again, with a new computer and a new apartment. But starting over was tiring. It was its own job and it was getting old. Also, and worst of all, Michael was sure Noah would outlive his every attempt at reinvention, however many there might be. He nearly had already. When the time came, Noah would survive Michael's wearing down, his giving up, and one day, if one of them were to stand above the grave of the other, it would not likely be Michael who was standing.

No! It couldn't have just been a relationship that ended badly, as so many do. It had to be something worse. It had to erase a twenty-year career from the middle of a man's life and then beguile him to, at any moment, take away all of what remained, including the freedom to start again. There are no ill-fated accusers, only the ill-fated accused.

"God—I hate you so much!" Michael raged through the room. If there had been anything there of less value than a laptop, he would have hurled it against the wall or through the open window. "I hate you so fucking much! I hate you so fucking much!" he yelled again and again and again, until he no longer understood that it wasn't himself he was telling.

Of All the Things I'm Wrong About

IT WAS THE TUESDAY before Thanksgiving, and I had arrived mid-morning for my first visit home from college. I'm lucky to go to college, since my family has never had much money; yet we're by no means poor or even conspicuously middleclass.

When I was I high school, my father's job as a CPA sustained us, while my mother's part-time job as a substitute teacher widened the gaps between needing to cut coupons versus not, shorter vacations versus longer, and store-brand snacks versus whatever fancy brand their hearts desired. It did not make such a difference, however, that my college choice was dictated by anything other than the best scholarship I could get. So, Wheaton College it was, in the Chicago suburbs, one hundred twenty-five miles from my hometown of Bloomington-Normal.

Cory, a sophomore and my coworker at Cap & Gown Books, had warned me to be on guard against what he called "the acute onset of holiday malaise." A New Testament studies major who smokes a lot of weed, Cory translated the condition into Latin, *"domesticus lassitudinensis,"* vesting it with the gravitas of a dead language. That was on Monday, the day before I left campus.

"It's a short visit," I had said.

"Before the turkey's thawed," he prophesied, "you'll be angling for an excuse to get out of the house. Before the first box-store opens, you'll be hooking up online. Before the cock crows three times on Black Friday," he said, "if you're not careful, you'll have said things to your parents that could get you disowned. When do you come back?"

"Sunday," I said.

"Oh," Cory said. "A whole week."

"It's five days."

"Do your parents pay your tuition?"

"I'm on a partial scholarship," I said.

As an only child, I always felt like the object of undue attention, and especially from my mother, whom I have reason to believe lost a child on her first go-round. It's not something we talk about, and in my family, there has always been much to guess at. One thing I didn't need to guess at is how my parents would fare better with me out of the house.

Together, my scholarship and part-time job made up the difference (and then some) between money they had saved for my college and the cost of tuition. This meant the money they had been spending on Catholic school tuition, about eight grand a year, would go to their bottom line. And there would be other savings. Money for food and clothes and the incidental costs that children bring would all come back to them as they sailed their ship west, its load lightened, toward retirement.

But it wasn't only about the money. I was equally sure my parents, and especially my mother, worried less about me since I'd left. Something about my being out from under her roof, I sensed, brought relief. It was as if she knew she had done her part and was now absolved of responsibilities where I was concerned. While a few of my friends' mothers had cried when they left home, my mother blessed me with a kiss on the forehead and sent me away with what sounded like a sigh of relief. No sooner had I returned than her stress did, too.

After a nap, I went downstairs for food. I'm not sure why it felt like sneaking, except I was moving fast and becoming increasingly frustrated to remember my mother's habit of always having a ton of food in the house but never anything to eat.

24

Cupboard shelves were jammed back-to-front with spices, canned goods, and other non-perishables. In the fridge were weird cheeses she liked to try, alongside near-empty containers of milk, juice, and pop. I had returned to the cupboard and was pulling out an unopened box of Save Rite crackers when she came in.

"Are you looking for something?"

"Just anything," I said. My mom took the box from me.

"If you're hungry," she said, "just ask."

"I am hungry," I said.

"You'll spoil your dinner," she said, putting the crackers away.

"It's not even three."

"We're eating early," she said, "and you father insists on taking us out."

"So, I'm not supposed to eat?"

"You can do whatever you want, Quinton. You always have."

"What's that supposed to mean?"

"Never mind," she said. My mother left the room and I wondered if, six hours into my first visit home, the opening salvos in my disowning had already been fired.

We ate in. My parents had pizza delivered, which told me they had argued about going out and my mother had won. From the time we sat down, the audio alert from my phone's messenger went off four times. Halfway through dinner, I was low-key spooked at how right Cory had been, as I began to contemplate hooking up online.

"Quinton," my father said stoically, his hands meeting above the table, "we have some bad news." My mother, who had not stopped seeming upset since the episode in the kitchen, left the table to refill our glasses. When she returned, my father continued.

"I lost my job," he said.

"No way," I said. "You've been there forever." My mother, lips pursed, nodded. "I mean, aren't you close to retirement anyway?"

"Not close enough," she said. "Not nearly close enough."

"The timing's not great," Dad said. "Markets are down. Ironically, this would be a good time to be putting money into the IRA." His tone suggested they had already started taking money out of it.

"How *could* they," my mother snarled, ready to relitigate an episode I was so glad to have missed. "After all you've done for them!"

"Amanda," Dad said. He looked at me. "It will mean some changes. Mostly on our end. But we thought you should know."

"Of course," I said. "I'll do anything I can to help."

"It would help," he said, "if you picked up the cost of your wireless plan."

"You can keep your number," my mother was quick to add. Around the time I had left for school, she learned to text. If practice makes perfect, my mom seemed to be aiming at perfection. She was constantly sending me quirky comments that were never questions and rants about people she thought I knew or cared about. By Halloween, and on a near-daily basis, my phone would suddenly begin beeping with the frenzied distress signal of a sinking ship. That was when I switched her number to "do not disturb."

"All right," I said. "If there's anything else . . . like school?"

"There's nothing else," Mom said, her eyes diving from the table.

"There's nothing else right now," Dad said.

26

In my room, from my phone, I went on Grindr. That's when it occurred to me the power it brought, and since it was, in fact, now *my* phone. I was beyond audit or examination, at once emancipated and advantaged. I held it in my hands like a shiny, black heart, or a thousand hearts, or a million.

Before my brush with Cory's wisdom, I had pondered Thanksgiving break as an opportunity to come out to my parents as bisexual. When I guessed at downsides, I imagined things like my mother deciding they would no longer pay my wireless bill. I doubt I would have done it in any case, and I certainly wasn't going to after hearing my father's news.

In the bathroom, I lifted the front of my shirt over my head and hooked it behind my neck to take a new picture—headless, of my torso. No freshman fifteen for me. If anything, I had lost a pound or two from an already skinny frame.

The first time I hooked up I used a headless photo to guard my identity. I continued to do this, though less for that reason than because I believe we are more attractive in the imagination of others than we are likely to be in reality—even me, who's attractive by ordinary standards. The first time I hooked up I was terrified. And yet that was why I did it. Apart from liking sex, I did it for the thrill. I did it as an exercise of power. I did it because I could. For whatever other reasons I might have done it, I didn't do it for the hundred-dollar bill the man gave me as I was leaving his apartment.

"I can't do this every time," he said, handing me the note as I stood at the door. I had not asked for money; I certainly had not negotiated an amount; and I had no expectation that there would be another time. Let alone an every time.

I never saw that guy again, even if in addition to the Benji he gave me much to think about on the walk home. Whether he was buying back his shame or tipping me; whether he was trying to get me on some kind of retainer or apologizing for not getting it up (or just what exactly) it didn't matter. No sooner was the cash spent than he was forgotten. What I didn't soon forget is how I have a moneymaker down there. Without trying, I had tapped into the real and unexpected value of disposable love.

When I got home that first night, I sneaked back in. By the time I left for college, I was coming and going like I owned the place and as late as four a.m. No one sleeps more soundly than my mother, and if my father knew I sneaked out, I knew he didn't care. It became one more thing we don't talk about.

Online, words like "generous" and "helpful" acquired an exact subtext. I would say I was able to negotiate things like more money, weed, and Uber rides, except there was no negotiation. I had only to ask. And here's a myth debunked: it's dangerous. Oh, please. At least half the time there isn't even sex as I understand the word. Bloomington-Normal is a university town, full of professors. And professors are the best. Nicest guys in the world. Smart, quirky, and often with more money than they know what to do with. They adore me, I think, because I remind them of their students or, sometimes, a son.

From the summer, the only man I kept in contact with is a guy named Edward. He's a professor in his late thirties who, via Google docs, edits my papers for me. When I asked if it wouldn't be easier for him to write them, he said it probably would be but that he wouldn't be helping me then. On random Fridays, he PayPals me fifty bucks with a note to have a good weekend. It's nice. When I asked what's the catch, he only said he wanted to take me to dinner when I'm home on break. There was no talk of sex.

I slept in on Wednesday. Dragging through the kitchen mid-afternoon, I found my mom in the throes of a manic bout of pie making. Flour dusted the counter around scattered spices, dirty mixing bowls, and geometries of leftover dough that had been cut for crusts.

"You know," I said, thinking to be helpful, "they make pumpkin pie spice that has your cloves and nutmeg and all this stuff already together."

It was the wrong thing to say.

I left for the backyard, her braying voice following me out. If she had wanted my help, she never would have asked. If I had offered, she would have refused sweetly like the passive-aggressive champ she is. Nobody guards their claim to anger any better than my mother. I imagined Cory inventing a name for it. Functional dysfunction.

In the backyard, Dad was raking leaves.

"Need help?" I asked.

He arched his back, seeming oblivious to the work all around him. "No, I'm fine," he said. "I don't know if you saw, but the Fitzgeralds are replacing their driveway." The Fitzgeralds are our neighbors.

"Oh, yeah?"

"Not sure when we'll get to ours," he said. "It needs it."

If I was going to make good on my commitment to let Edward take me to dinner, I knew it needed to be either today or Saturday. On the day after Thanksgiving, my family has a tradition of volunteering at a coat drive to benefit families who have fallen on hard times. It's a day that ends with dinner out.

"So," I said, "I was thinking I might hang out with friends tonight."

"Oh," Dad said. "Did you run that by your mother?"

29

"Should I?"

"Well," he said, "I'm OK with it. But you've only been home for a day."

I was keen to point out it had been two days, technically, before catching the words in my mouth. "Well . . . right. I mean, I don't want her to get the wrong idea," I said, knowing how for her to get the right idea would be so much worse.

In our family, a successful holiday is measured by how firmly it remains anchored in the safe port of tradition. At Thanksgiving, this includes hosting my father's sister, her husband, and their kids, Nelson and Molly.

"Aunt Jennifer and Uncle Less don't know," Mom said as our guests were pulling into the driveway.

Nelson, who's a year younger than me, naturally wanted to hear about college, but not in that annoying way adults ask, at the table, with a stupid cadence to their voice. After dinner but before pie, as we always do, Nelson and I took Molly for a walk to Ewing Park, where in the fall there's a cinematic quality to the color and the cold. I told him what I thought he should know about college. Molly is seven and has Down's. A sure spot of sweetness in our extended family, if there's any part of any tradition I don't mind, it's the time Nelson and I spend with her.

When we returned to the house, kind words were said about the pies. Following dessert, Dad, Nelson, Molly, and I watched football, even though none of us—and my father least of all—cares. Aunt Jennifer and my mother cleaned up.

After my dad's sister's family left, a pall settled over the place, a silence as suspicious as the house was suspiciously clean.

"They know," my mother startled me, my phone in-hand, when she stuck her head into my room on her way to bed.

Finishing up at the coat drive, I asked where we would go for dinner.

"Home," Mom said obviously. "The leftovers aren't going to eat themselves."

"I'd like it if we could go out tomorrow night then," Dad tried.

"Even if we still have food? I don't see why we can't have turkey two nights in a row," she said. "Knock it all out before you drive Quinton back on Sunday."

"Three," Dad said. "Three nights in a row."

With my plans made for me, I sent Edward a text. He was cool about it and said he'd take me out over the longer winter break. He was almost too reasonable, like one who knows how to indulge a patience others can't afford.

And indeed, others were less willing to be put off. My phone had been blowing up all day with message alerts from those I had met online who were angling to connect. It wasn't a problem until the three of us were together at the table, picking through all of what remained of the leftovers. My mom grew conspicuously annoyed, shifting in her seat with each series of beeps.

Soon, she disappeared to the kitchen only to return a minute later as angry as I've ever seen her. As angry as I've ever seen anyone.

"What do you think?" she blasted, leaning at me over the table, like it was the only thing to hold her back. "That you can just cut me off?"

"Amanda!" my Dad said.

"Your phone," she said. "*Your* phone won't stop going off. But when I text you, not a sound!" I pulled the device from my pocket and saw three texts from her, all sent within the last sixty seconds. "It that it, Quinton?" she broke down. "That you think you can just cut me off?"

31

"No," I said, for a moment frozen in place.

"Amanda . . . please," my father said.

I managed to stand to retreat to my room.

"Is that what you think?" she cried after me.

The next morning, I waited for my father to come downstairs to drive me back to campus. The living room was cool and airless, still meticulously clean and with all the joy of a funeral parlor. I hadn't expected it, but my mom was with him.

"Your mother has something she wants to say," Dad said quietly. I was ready to hear her apology. And of all the things I'm wrong about.

"Quinton," she spoke with the control of one who had rehearsed something a bit too well. "In the years before you were born, I had abortions." It struck me I had never heard anyone speak of having an abortion in the plural—*abortions*. I didn't know what to say.

Her composure was short-lived. "Four," she said, lips quivering. My father put his arms around her.

"You mother's not well," he explained. "She's battled depression for years."

"I thought," she said through tears. "I thought I was doing better!"

"Hush," Dad said, whispering comfort. I understood how, in light of what she had said, no news of depression would be expected to shock me. "You are, dear," he said. "You are doing better."

I didn't want to stay. I didn't want to go.

"Quinton," he said, "why don't you wait in the car."

It was a raw November morning. Gray and grayer clouds gathered above the blackened trees. Through the chain-link fence beneath my bedroom window, the one that separates the

Fitzgeralds' property from ours, I saw their two dogs, one large one and one small, romping around like loutish children. The large one was sniffing up trouble, nudging at the bottommost bags of a concrete mix the contractors had dropped off. The small one darted back and forth along the fence, pining for attention.

On the ninety-minute drive to campus, my father told me about his plans for getting back on his feet. We talked about how school was going for me, and we talked about sports, which didn't feel as artificial as it would have once.

When I returned to the bookstore on Monday, Cory was there. He wanted to know how things had gone for me at home.

"It was like you said," I told him.

"Really?" He seemed surprised—the way we can be when we're right.

"Maybe not quite so bad," I said. "My family's not what I thought."

"Most fairy tales only ever end one way," Cory said, ramping up the gloom.

"With a happy ending?"

"No," he said. "That's fantasies you're thinking of."

A Ring of Fire

I

IN A PART OF TOWN where children rarely go, Judy Folk, a mother of three, went to see her mother at Friendship Estates. But she was late. It was Monday, and she usually dropped by on Saturdays or even as early as Friday afternoons to get it over with. When she visited during the week, it was Judy's habit to do so on her way home from Nagle Elementary, where she taught fourth grade, and on those days she felt she was tending to the needs of people near both ends of life's journey.

Although it was mid-August, Judy's mother's room was cool and dark. The blinds were closed and there was only the affected joy of silk flowers on a bedside table to cheer the place.

"People really came together during the war," the old woman said.

"What war's that?"

"The one . . . you know. Lots of people died," she said. "You're late."

"I know."

Judy was aware that her mother, who couldn't distinguish one war from another, refused to lose track of time. It was as if each calendar cell was a tether binding her to life. Occasionally, when she couldn't remember if she had crossed through the previous day, she called the local Hardee's to confirm the date. A nurse at Friendship Estates had told Judy that her mother did this.

"Does she annoy them?" Judy asked, as one who knew annoyance.

"I don't think so," the nurse said.

That's when Judy wondered—with some relief—why she didn't call her only daughter.

"It's Monday," her mother croaked.

"I couldn't make it this weekend," Judy said. "The kids . . . and Char." She wagged her head to think of her middle son, Charlie.

"Have you seen the paper?" said the old woman. "People really are coming together."

"What do you mean?"

"Like they did during the war."

On a table by the window, Judy spotted *The Tell City Telegraph*. The headline was all the news in town, which was all the news everywhere—news of the eclipse.

She read the first paragraph:

People are coming together, gathering in Tell City from across the nation and around the world in anticipation of next Monday's solar eclipse. With a magnitude of 1.0306, day will turn to night, and for two minutes and forty seconds the sun will appear as a ring of fire. It will be the first total eclipse visible in North America this century.

"Have the nurses been reading to you?"

"People really are coming together," her mother repeated, with a prophet's gloom.

Judy opened the blinds, sending a cosmos of dust tumbling through the air. She turned to her mother, who lay thin and neatly folded into linens like a letter ready to be sent.

At forty-four, Judy was not thin. She had roomy hips, large breasts, and a full, round face that was the portrait of a slow-waning beauty. But it was stress that was stealing from her the best of what remained. Lately, she found herself on the receiving end of all things—surrounded by catheter tubes and heart monitors at the nursing home and, at her home, by the sass of post-pubescence and a middle boy she was sure took drugs and was selling body to pay for them.

An orderly arrived to deliver snacks. He looked about nineteen, the age of Judy's oldest son, Mark. He had Mark's eyes, bright and kind, she was noticing, when her mother intruded on her thoughts.

"May I have two peanut butter cookies, or do I have to choose two different kinds?"

"You can have two of whatever kind you like," the boy said.

He set a box of juice on the tray-table. Like her boys, the orderly was more pretty than handsome. Unlike her boys, he had a job.

After he left, Judy stood by—trying to keep crumbs out of the sheets.

"Now, Mom, what sort of question was that?"

"What?"

"About the cookies," Judy said. "What sort of question was that?"

"I like peanut butter," she said.

"Why would you think you couldn't have two?"

"Other people might like peanut butter."

Leave it to her mother, Judy thought, to shame her by considering others. When her children shamed her, it wasn't like this. She drove a straw through the top of the juice box.

"What if it rains?" The old woman chewed while she spoke.

"It's sunny enough."

"On the twenty-first. For the eclipse," she said. "What if it's cloudy?"

Judy had thought of this. "There'll still be an eclipse," she said, wiping her mother's face.

"How can you say that?"

"The eclipse is still there. Just because all these people can't see it."

Her mother's face soured.

Judy knew she couldn't have been more cynical if she had told the old woman that, by the same logic, the gates of heaven stand open and ready—just because all these people can't see it. "Anyhow," Judy said, "it's sunny enough today."

"Today is not a week from today."

"No, it's not," she said, looking at the calendar. The current day's date, August 14th, had already been crossed through. In the cell directly beneath it, Monday, August 21st, there was nothing to note the eclipse.

Judy pinched together several more crumbs from the pillowcase and urged her mother, who looked sleepy, to drink her juice. And what if she should forget, Judy imagined, or sleep through it? What if it fell to her to describe how miraculous it had been? It would be one more way in which the elderly weary the young without even trying.

On the drive home, Judy thought mostly of her mother and Char. She refused to think of the woman as dying. Dying people die, and at eighty-seven there was no indication her mother planned to deliver on such a promise.

And Char. God, Char.

Sometimes Judy allowed herself to admit that she dreaded to be in the boy's presence and that it was satisfying enough to experience her children, all three of them, as she preferred them to be rather than as she was forced to see them. Char, who had recently turned seventeen, had fallen beyond her sphere of influence. His older and younger brothers, Mark and Ed, offered no more trouble than help, and yet she guessed they conspired

38

with him to deceive her. Her husband, Paul, was often gone for work but was lax with the boys when he was around, confirming Judy's role as a woman in it alone.

Clouds gathered west of Tell City, a stratocumulus patchwork through which Jesus rays, as her church friends called them, shown down. To get caught in a storm would be just the thing, Judy thought, in their convertible with the leaky top. Paul, who drove the Lexis for business trips, insisted that their second car, a '97 Mustang, be fun, even if his idea of fun was her idea of a gas-guzzler they could only drive in dry weather.

"This family deserves its fun," Paul was fond of saying. As lightning flickered in the distance, Judy wondered what that meant for her. The fun they deserved also included family vacations and, two years earlier, a cruise on which Mark and Char vowed openly to lose their virginity and Ed had to be rushed to the ship's hospital after taking Xanax he had gotten from his brothers.

What family? Judy thought. What fun?

But if her mother could run out the clock, then so could she. Ed would turn eighteen in less than three years, and when the nest was empty there would be time for her and Paul—or time for her alone—to move on.

II

Mark and Ed were attractive and straight. Shiftless by nature, they were lazy about school. Char, on the other hand, was stunning and gay. By far the cleverest of the three, he was also bold and as likely to spend the night away from home as not. Judy had stopped pretending to care that her two oldest boys got high and snuck beer. With Char, however, there were things she couldn't overlook: Designer briefs in the laundry. Expensive sunglasses he no longer tried to hide. Money he had. When he was gone, she guessed, he disabled his phone so as not to be found. When he was home, she would take it, if she could, and retreat to the bathroom to read messages he was too careless to delete.

Ahead of her, Saint Joseph's Catholic Church came into view. It was Judy's church, a small, modern structure halfway between Friendship Estates and home. For nine months she had been attending fellowship meetings. The women of St. Joe's were as glad to have her as they were to commiserate—even if that's all it was, a sharing of miseries. There were no shared strategies for reigning in a promiscuous teen, dealing with a parent's dementia, or dealing with the guilt of not wanting to deal with it. Instead, recipes for banana bread were exchanged. There was prayer, talk of the power of prayer, and talk of mysteries. It was here Judy heard the most about the eclipse. Discussions were had concerning what, if anything, to do about it.

"Do about it?" Nancy Bergman had said at the last meeting.

"Well," Linda Perret clarified, "should we talk it up . . . celebrate it?"

Ellie Baker suggested they ask Father to organize a special mass. Jan Hibbard wanted a viewing party. Pam Morrison got creative and suggested a large-scale renewal of marriage vows, as a compromise between the secular and the holy.

Judy, whose turn was next, had it in mind to say "or a large-scale suicide" before settling on "I like the viewing party idea. We could have a picnic."

With such considerations came details of the big day. Some of the women had even arranged to let spare rooms in their homes, but Paul would never allow strangers in the house. Besides, Judy knew, there could be no better guarantee Char would want to spend the night at home than to rent his room.

The women spoke of the eclipse like experts, and Judy left meetings knowing more than she cared to.

"The center will be over Orchard Dale Farm. Do you think we should have the picnic there?" Jan asked, as if Judy's idea had been agreed to.

"I don't see the point," Pam said. "It'll be a madhouse. We're in the band of totality. Let the world come to us for a change."

"Like it won't be a madhouse here?" Nancy said. "Do you know how many people live in Tell City? Seven thousand, seven hundred and seventy-nine. Do you know how many people will be here for the eclipse? Upwards of twenty thousand!"

This latter number had been bandied about, but no one could explain to Judy where it came from. What she did know was that the first day of school, Monday, August 21st, had been pushed back to Tuesday, August 22nd. It would mean an extra day of summer vacation, an extra day without children, which, as far as Judy was concerned, was reason enough to give thanks to the universe.

Minutes before the sky opened, Judy arrived to what she thought was an empty house. The living room was like an icebox, still her face blistered with frustration that the boys would have left without turning off the air. In the kitchen, the oven was on and with the door cracked. The freezer door was ajar.

"Char!" Judy snapped. She turned off the oven and closed the freezer. "Why is the oven on?"

"I'm making corndogs." It was Ed's voice, coming from his basement room.

"Three minutes in the microwave," she yelled.

"They're frozen," he said on his way up.

"Three minutes in the microwave will do it."

"Char's gone." Ed appeared in the threshold. Sluggish, he wore only a pair of purple Raisin Bran boxers with a buoyant cartoon sun grinning across the fly. The sun's rays were flaccid, like tentacles on an anemone.

Two small hands, attached to a girl shorter than Ed, snaked around his torso, moving him to one side so she could pass. She was dressed and appeared to be leaving.

"I don't need a corndog," the girl said.

"Hello," Judy said, resting her hands on her hips.

"Hello," the girl said pleasantly. She showed herself out through the den, where, unless Mark was watching, the television had been left on.

"Where's Mark?"

"Gone."

"And Char?"

"He doesn't live here anymore," Ed explained. "The thing is, they're crispier when you make 'em in the oven."

"What do you mean Char doesn't live here anymore?" She took a plate from the cupboard, arranged the corndogs side-by-side, and put the plate into the microwave.

Ed took a seat at the table.

When Judy went into the den to turn off the television, there was breaking news on about a well-known character actor who, according to his publicist, had passed away. The boys wouldn't have heard of him, but he had been a big star on several sitcoms in the late eighties, and people knew his face.

Back in the kitchen, Judy asked again, but this time as one more concerned than curious. "What do you mean Char doesn't live here anymore?" She knew better than to ask Ed to put on clothes. His body was lean and toned, although he had never seen the inside of a gym and he ate corndogs like a condemned man.

"I don't know," Ed said. "Did you set a timer?"

42

"Huh?"

"For the food."

"No." Judy sat across from him. "It's three minutes more or less."

"When's Dad coming home?"

"I don't know," she said. "Did you set a timer? I'll ask you one more time. What do you mean Char doesn't live here anymore?"

"I don't know!" Ed said. "I'm sorry I said anything. It's on Facebook."

"You know he blocked me."

"How would I know that?" Ed seemed to be deciding if the wait for food was worth the examination. "He met some old guy. Says he's forty. Drives a Benz."

"Forty!"

"I don't know," Ed said. "He's old."

"Well, I hope Char's happy." Judy pushed back from the table. "Maybe we can have lunch sometime."

"You're not mad?"

Judy went upstairs and checked Char's bedroom on the way to her own. Some of his things—a laptop, a few posters, and some clothes—were gone. What was she going to do, she thought, call the police? And tell them what, that her seventeen-year-old son has found a sugar daddy? When Judy got to her computer, she logged on to Facebook using Mark's password, which she had obtained by stealth.

"mooooved to the city, niggahz!!" was Char's most recent post. As best she could tell, this meant Louisville, where someone named David Kainet had tagged her son in a photo outside of the Speed Art Museum.

She read on.

David was not forty. He was forty-four, her age, but he looked younger. He was an investment banker who had traveled in Rome, Berlin, London, and who did, as Ed reported, drive a Benz. What Ed would not have said, but what Judy noticed immediately, was that the man was remarkably handsome. His hair was full and brown. He was tall, slim, and his eyes shone childishly, like they belonged to someone still believing there could be any joy in life.

Air hissed from the vent above, and the back of Judy's neck grew cold. She shuttered to imagine an existence where knowledge of her son would come, coarse-grained, from a series of status updates. A crude, digital legacy. She scrolled through more of David's photos, entertaining a universe in which he could be, at the same time, Char's lover and her own. When she had had enough, she forced her attention briefly to an online discussion of the dead character actor's legacy.

On her way back to the kitchen, Judy held the rail, as her mother had when she was still able to take stairs. What would her friends at St. Joe's think of it, she wondered, if she so freely released her middle boy to the world? What they would say (to her at least) would not be what they would think.

Downstairs, the smell of burnt batter filled the rooms. Ed had taken his food from the microwave and put it back into the oven. In the kitchen, a pall of smoke hovered near the ceiling, and at the table Ed was finishing off the last corndog. The edges of his mouth were stained with catsup as he took the last two bites and discarded the charred wooden stick on top of the rest.

"Sorry," he said, retreating to his lair.

Whatever Ed was sorry for—having a girl over, using the oven, burning the food, eating it all himself, or breaking the news about his brother—to Judy, sinking back into her chair, it couldn't have mattered less.

II

By Friday, August 18th, weather forecasts from the Pacific Northwest to the southeast coast were getting considerable attention. By Sunday, the search for clarity was manic. Travel plans were made or changed. In Vegas, wagers were taken. On the drive to see her mother, Judy imagined a scene in New York with conference-room tables flanked by news executives discussing how best to put their cameras into the eclipse's path.

In Tell City, the afternoon was sunny and hot. Similar conditions had been forecasted for the days ahead. For those determined to find the darkness by seeking out the light, there could be no better place, Judy knew, than in her shoes.

"Tomorrow's the big day!" her mother said. The staff at Friendship Estates wore purposeful expressions. Engaged in a dry run, they were wheeling residents into rows along the western patio.

A nurse swept by with a box of eclipse glasses, announcing with every pair that left her hands, "Practice putting these on, but we must have them back." Most complied, and it was quite a sight, Judy thought, this phalanx of geriatric badasses, some huddled under blankets in ninety-degree heat. Only one or two refused to put the glasses on; they were told that, unless they did, they would not be allowed to watch tomorrow. The man parked next to Judy's mother appeared to be eating his.

"I never thought I'd live to see this," her mother said. "If you had asked me thirty years ago, I wouldn't have thought I'd live to see the year 2000. But this—this is the icing on the cake. Judy? Where are you?"

"Right here." From behind, Judy leaned over the wheelchair. She wondered if her mother reasoned that, by virtue of having lived so long, she was somehow guaranteed even one more day of life. "I don't see the big deal," she said. "There's another one in 2024."

"What's that?" her mother looked up through the dark glasses like a wild, bug-eyed alien.

"Nothing," Judy said. "Never mind."

"Will you come tomorrow?" she said. "It's Monday. The day of the moon. They've canceled school. Will you come tomorrow and bring the children? The family should be together in case we meet God." Judy rolled her eyes. "The man down the hall, Mr. Fleener, says we're going to meet God."

"I don't know Mr. Fleener," Judy said, "and I can't meet God tomorrow. Our church group is having a picnic. Besides, I'm sure you'd rather be with your friends."

Judy watched as the same nurse who had passed out the glasses brushed by to collect them, removing some directly from the residents' faces. Although she didn't hesitate to take the pair from the hands of the man next to them, the frames of which glistened with drool, she did pause long enough to attach a red tag to the handle on his wheelchair: NO ECLIPSE.

The next morning the country seemed to hold its breath in anticipation of an event mystical, yet known. At 10:15, on a strand north of Newport, Oregon, the moon's shadow touched US soil. Judy watched and listened as news anchors hushed and a near-silent crowd basked in the umbra for one minute and fifty-five seconds. Then, as slowly as it had beset them, the arc pulled away and the multitude exploded into cheers, as if delivered through a great ordeal.

Judy turned off the television. Once and for all she had to decide whether to drink the Kool-Aid with her mother at Friendship Estates or with her friends at Orchard Dale Farm.

46

The old folks' home would be more amusing, but better to be with the church crowd, she figured, where her kids would not be expected than with family where they would be missed. Not even Paul, who was in Chicago for the week, cared to see the eclipse. When Judy had tested, trying to get him to admit that it at least sounded interesting, he only said it was not his idea of fun.

Ed was asleep downstairs. Except to rouse him, he was the only one of her boys over whom Judy felt she had control. Char was in Louisville, and Mark had spent the night with his friend, Trevor. According to Facebook, they were meeting others the night before "to get eclipsed" at a party in the country.

By the time she left for Orchard Dale Farm, the moon was passing over Idaho and Wyoming on its way to Nebraska.

Judy crossed the Ohio River into Kentucky, where briefly she thought of Char. A half-hour south of the Hoosier National Forest, her phone rang. Had the kids been with her, Judy would have made a point not to answer while driving. But she was already late.

"Hello?"

"May I speak to Judy Folk?" a man said. The voice was unfamiliar, and she wondered if this might be David Kainet calling to offer to return her son.

"This is Judy," she said. "Who's this?"

"Mrs. Folk, I'm Lieutenant Mason of the Tell City Police."

"What's wrong?" Judy slowed to veer off the highway.

"There's been an incident," he said. "I need you to come to the station."

"What happened? How did you get this number?"

"I don't have all the details, but we called your home and your son—"

"Ed?"

"Yes, ma'am," the officer said. "He gave me the number."

47

"What happened?"

"There's been an incident involving your other son."

"Charlie?"

"No, ma'am."

"Mark?"

"Yes, ma'am," he said. "Your husband is out of town. Is that correct?"

"Yes." Mindless of the traffic, Judy turned the car around. "What happened?"

"I need you to come as soon as you can," he said. "If you can't drive, I can send someone."

"Of course I can drive," Judy said. "I'm driving now. Where am I driving to?"

"The station on Mozart. Do you know—?"

"I know where it is. But I insist on knowing—"

"Mrs. Folk, everything will be all right. But if you can't drive safely—"

"I'm fine to drive," she said, trading anxiety for anger to imagine whatever trouble Mark had gotten into. "I'll be there as soon as I can."

Judy gripped the wheel. For twenty minutes she sped in silence, wondering why—if everything would be all right, as the lieutenant had said—he was concerned about her driving. As she approached the Hoosier National Forest a second time, Judy turned on the radio to distract herself and follow the progress of the eclipse. The first news she heard were details of the character actor's funeral, which had happened the previous day. Thanks were given for a full life, lived by one whose legacy was the enduring joy he had brought to many.

At 1:22, the eclipse was said to be racing over Paducah at the speed of sound. On both sides of the highway, Judy saw people exiting cars and campers that lined Route 166. At 1:25, her phone rang again. This time Judy drove the Mustang onto the shoulder before answering.

"Hello?" There was the sound of labored breathing, distant but familiar. "Ed?"

Judy turned off the radio. She turned off the engine and sat forward.

"Mom?" Ed was sobbing, a sound she hadn't heard in years.

"What happened?"

"It's Mark."

"What about Mark?" Judy exited the car and walked to the edge of the woods.

"The police called. They wouldn't say."

As Judy came under the cover of trees, birds went silent. "Ed, you tell me what you know this instant!"

"Trevor's mom called," he said. "Mark and him. There was an accident." It seemed to Judy that neither of them could stand the sound of his voice. "It was bad."

"Ed!"

"They're dead," he said. "She said . . . she said . . ."

A bolt of light seemed to flash from behind her eyes. Judy's legs buckled. As she lowered her hand, the phone fell from it. A breeze stirred, and she was aware of the falling temperature. Judy stumbled forward, as awkward as a child, and could hear some of the cars honking their horns. She put her hands over her ears, taking a few more steps before she tripped and fell.

For an awful moment, Judy saw her mother at Friendship Estates—one among many in a long queue of grotesque survivors, groping chair-to-chair for a partner's hand. At Orchard Dale Farm, her vision was of friends, in contest over who could seem most capable of wonder. Judy shut her eyes, to see her grief and cheat herself of life's novelty, but all she could see was Mark at each stage of his ordinary life. She could not recall the last time she had seen him, but knew she could not bear to look at him again.

When she opened her eyes, dark films had fallen in around her. Rising at the knees, Judy felt as one cleaved from her body, a separate self, yet not so much a self as a shadow of that, like one who had labored to bring great beauty into the world but who now, with her work finished, was being called back to the night.

Her skin grew numb, and for a moment it was fine to be alone—and less than alone—as it must have been before life began. To inhabit a place where moons, and stars, and planets continually cross paths with no one there to know.

The Conventioneer

I

IT CAME DOWN TO NEEDING to decide between the ophthalmologists and Pinball International's Mechanized Play Society. I chose the PIMPS. I had gone against instincts before and been rewarded, most notably the time I passed on International Mister Leather in favor of NASA—the North American Schooners Association. Then, I woke up in the dark on a Monday afternoon. I didn't know it was Monday or afternoon at the time. I was naked in the hull of a small yacht, on my back and trussed to a broken-off section of mast. I would later discover we were adrift on Lake Michigan, two miles from Chicago's Navy Pier. With my eyes wide open, all was blackness. My body rolled by the motions of the boat, and the only sound was the mid-pitched ding of metal on metal from on deck.

Bilge water—or some kind of water—passed between my shoulders and the floor. A smell like chub mixed with gasoline burned my sinuses. Had we gone fishing? I was sure we had not.

The fumes' boozy effect made the pain in my head worse, and the irregular clang of the metal grew steadily more annoying. From experience, I knew I would feel better if I could make myself throw up. Soon, a quake gathered in the pit of my gut— too late to halt the inevitable by the time I realized I wasn't able to tilt my head fully to either side.

I arched my back and heaved. With my tongue, I emptied the pockets of both cheeks before sipping in enough air to blow out whatever else I could ahead of the next wave. Tears rolled down my temples and into my ears. When it was over, I did feel better and I knew then it wasn't chub I smelled.

I also knew not to yell for help. There had been three of us the night before. I remembered how the other two, the man who owned the yacht and a woman we'd met, made it clear the only way to be sure I *wouldn't* get untied was to yell for help. If I said "Yes, sir" to him, the woman walloped my balls with her open palm. If I said "Yes, ma'am" to her, the man cracked me across the jaw with his fist.

After this, I recalled nothing much.

Again, from experience, I knew it would help if I closed my eyes and concentrated on my breathing. When I opened them again it was to the sound of someone unfastening the galley's hatch.

A flood of light filled the narrow cabin, into which the man climbed down. He was pencil-thin in silhouette.

"Jee-zus," he said. "What's that smell?" His voice was unsteady. His hands, too, as he unfastened the knots he had made. That's when I remembered why I had chosen the yachtsmen over the leather daddies. Since I wanted to be tied up, I was determined it should be done by one who knew their craft and not some weekend warrior, whose idea of bondage is a way to make use of unwanted neckties.

Topside, day faded and the man rigged a sail to bring us in. The vessel was a wreck, where both the mainsheet and clew had broken loose from the boom. But if it didn't bother him, it didn't bother me. He stayed back to mind the tiller. I stood at the bow, beneath the mad trill of a backstay fluttering in the wind. Empty beer bottles warbled across the deck, some careening into the sides of the yacht and vaulting overboard like an escaped fish.

The man looked as shiny yet as bloodless as a gutted fish. He seemed not to want to look at me. We didn't speak before arriving at an abandoned jetty, one-quarter mile south of the Fifty-Seventh Street Beach. As light left the sky, a haze came between us. The man had lost all confidence from the night before. He was in a fretful hurry to moor the boat and motion me off it.

"Wasn't there someone with us?" I asked, stepping onto the pier. "A woman?"

"No," he said.

"Someone we met at the venue," I said. "She was from Canada." I felt the charge of one overly empowered, like someone who ties up a stranger and threatens them not to yell for help. The man had, quite definitely, the look of one tied.

"Now see here," he said, the vessel already separating from the landing. "We were the only ones."

"Her name was Maria . . . or Marissa."

"See here!" he cried, sailing east into the new night. "It was just us out there!"

Where there are doctors, there are drugs. Pharmaceutical reps, however, never seem to have them. They have pens and cheaply bound notepads for the doctors, who are always the ones with the drugs. If you want to get laid, crash a convention of media types (so insecure). If you want insider-trading tips, you might think investors, right? Wrong. Computer programmers. If it's real estate knowledge you seek, as opposed to a good time, realtors are indeed the way to go. But the conventions I most enjoy are those I know the least about, like the time I crashed the Illinois Classical Studies Conference and got blitzed with a clutch of high school Latin teachers. This was one reason I chose Pinball International's Mechanized Play Society over the ophthalmologists, who are doctors and have drugs. Yes, even the ophthalmologists.

The PIMPS were meeting Thursday through Sunday at the Palmer House, which was the other reason I chose them. I hadn't been to that hotel in over a year, and I'm careful not to be familiar. Another plus: the place is grand. Too grand for old-school gamers, I thought in the cab on my way to the Loop. Because I live in town, I never book a room. My m.o. is to buy a single-day, at-large registration, when available, and to acquire the legitimacy of a nametag if not also a lanyard. I've collected more than a few. If the convention is more professional than recreational, the venue's bar, which is open to all, is a good place to start. And Saturday night is the time to go, when the formalities are finished and people are more likely to take that deep dive to test the limits of their second selves.

No matter their stripe, conventioneers mostly have this in common: they are there, in an alien city among fellow aliens, ostensibly for one thing and less ostensibly for another. They talk of it openly to strangers, at least, but occasionally among themselves, as a kind of free vacation. "What happens in Vegas stays in Vegas" does not only apply to Vegas.

I entered the wide, gilded lobby, which I was amused to find flanked by no fewer than fifty pinball machines. It was a carnival of bells and whistles, hardly different from any casino boat I've ever been on. Crystal chandeliers wept light from parquet ceilings. The dull glow of three evenly spaced banker's lamps pooled across the surface of a mahogany registration desk, which I passed on my way to the table that would have my packet and nametag.

Some of the smaller rooms were reserved for vintage games. Foosball . . . plinko. But the pinball machines, the stars of the show, were on full display. For fear of losing repeat business, venues allow organizers get away with a lot. Every machine had been programmed for unlimited free plays, and while many were occupied, *Elvira*, *Indiana Jones and the Temple of Doom* and *Super Mario Bros Mushroom World* were available. But it was *Twenty Thousand Leagues Under the Sea* that caught my eye and the one I paused to play. I'm never in a rush. This is my downtime. Other people take vacations. I do this.

"You must be Nathan," Beth Ann said as I approached the table, reaching for the printout of my online registration.

"How did you know?" I knew how she knew.

"Well, you could be Cindy . . . Shannon or Holly, but I doubt it."

"For a moment, I thought you were clairvoyant," I said.

"Nope. I'm Beth Ann." Beth Ann struck me as the administrative sort, clinically dependable and trustworthy to a fault. If you were to go on vacation, your plants would have no better caretaker, your pet no more attentive companion. I wondered who was caring for her plants and attending to her pet.

"As it turns out, I am Nathan," I said, producing the paperwork. My name is not Nathan.

"Better late than never," she said, checking the form against a master list and then passing me my nametag. "You write for *Popular Mechanics*," she observed.

"Freelance," I said. "I'm here to do a feature."

"Are you sure you're not a famous writer?" Beth Ann said, winking at me above the top of her glasses. "I can introduce you to some people . . . for your story." In her eyes, I saw a look I knew. An interest in being more than helpful. She was short and somewhat chunky, perhaps in her late fifties. Her complexion was raw, her skin dotted with moles. Beth Ann's posture was poor in a way to suggest she was weighed down by something more than weight.

"I might take you up on that," I said. "But let me wander around first, to get the lay of the land."

"Suit yourself," she said. "But don't miss the dance at ten o'clock in the Paris Room. It's the big send off."

"I may be late to the party," I said, "but I won't be late to that party."

I wouldn't have gone to the Paris Room even if I had not known Beth Ann would be there, hoping to write a grand conclusion to her weekend. When they have them, dances are for the conventional conventioneers, and I've found it's hard to hear and be heard above the music.

I tried my hand at several more games of pinball. I had no chance of setting a high score, and besides, when something is free it ultimately feels like a thing not worth doing.

"You're terrible!" came a voice so close it could have been my own. I was back playing *Twenty Thousand Leagues Under the Sea*, thinking of Maria—or Marissa? at the bottom of Lake Michigan. A teenage boy, rail-thin and slightly taller than me, glowered over my shoulder. "You're the worst player I've ever seen." He said it with such conviction, I wondered if it was something I ought to be proud of.

"Is that your thing?" I said. "To sneak up on people?"

"I've been here for like five minutes," he said. The boy's skin was smooth. His face paper-white. Thick black bangs crested above a pair of deep-green, olive-shaped eyes. He was either too stupid or had been too long among his fellow enthusiasts to take offense.

"Are you waiting to play or . . . just what exactly?" I said.

"Just watching," he said. "You can learn a lot by watching."

"And what have you learned?"

"That you're a terrible player," he said.

56

"That's because I'm not a player," I said, leaving the console but turning in a direction that allowed him glean my nametag and affiliation. "I'm a writer."

"Oh," Zac said. His nametag had tiny, multi-colored cannabis leaves drawn on it. "Makes sense. Sorry, man. I didn't mean to steal your chill."

I made for the bar without another word to Zac, shaking my head and wondering how exactly one steals another's chill.

For the occasion, I was Nathan Schiff, forty-two, a writer working on a piece for *Popular Mechanics'* retro issue due out in the winter. For the occasion, as for previous ones, I had grown up in the Chicago suburbs but lived in New York City since college. "In New York, you can work your tail off or do practically nothing and somehow still seem busy," I like to say. It's my favorite line. It makes me seem mysterious yet forthcoming, driven yet not self-important, urbane yet accessible. It allows me to be, at the start of most conversations, whomever anyone needs me to be.

And the rest, that's the fun part. Grafting a narrative onto other people's stories—their fears, expectations, desires. I'm a great listener. To indulge a vanity, all the best liars are great listeners.

But God save me from these PIMPS, I thought. They were the sorriest, safest, saddest group I had seen in years. As soon as I mentioned New York, one woman, Lynnette, from Bulls Gap, Tennessee, started crying. Her husband had run off with a Starbucks barista half his age, "—to New York, or L.A. or Tampa or one-a them cities," she sobbed. All I could think was who cries at a pinball convention. "I haf s'pected to see one-r both uv 'om here," she blathered. "There's a Starbucks on damn near every corner!" Lynnette fell into a fresh fit, burying her face in her hands. "If I'd only knew!" she bawled. "I woodn'ta even came!"

Moving on.

Drunk. Drunk. Unhinged. Dull. Virtuous. Dull. Extremely drunk. Dull.

I briefly considered trying to find Zac, before deciding if I heard one more "tilt" joke I would call it a night.

Then I remembered Beth Ann.

II

"I lied!"

"There you are!" Beth Ann said, dialing up her voice above the music. "What did you say?"

"I said I lied, and I'm sorry! I told you I wouldn't be late!"

"Let's go outside!" she said. "I can't hear myself think!"

Through the Paris Room's double doors, the world fell silent. The pinball machines, running the length of the lobby on both sides, stood mute and unattended like rows of electric coffins.

"Honestly," I said, "I don't think I've ever seen someone take their purse to a dance." Beth Ann's right hand clutched the top of a large bag, which she wore like a sling over her left shoulder.

"I couldn't see leaving it in the room," she said. "I've read about the crime in Chicago." The bag was sheeny, white, and decorated with splatters of red, yellow, and orange that might have been flowers but looked more like a lost game of paintball. A woman, drunk, lolled out of the Paris Room after us and began to paw at Beth Ann's shoulder.

"I thawt that that was yew," she said, patting herself down before coming up with a fistful of cash from a front pocket. "I told you I had it," she said. "I *told* you!" The woman opened Beth

Ann's purse and shoved the money in. "Fiftee!" she said. "Count it yerself, if you don't truss me."

"I'm in charge of the door money," Beth Ann explained as we walked away. "And the money from all these people who never pay dues until the last minute."

"Really?" I said.

"I'm a nervous wreck carrying it around."

"Chicago's not as dangerous as all that," I said.

"Are you from here?"

"I grew up in the suburbs," I said, "but I've lived in New York since college. You know, it's nice out and not so late I can't show you the downtown lights."

"I'm not sure," Beth Ann said.

"You can see the best parts of the city from a ride on the el."

"It's like you read my mind!" she said. "I've been dying to experience the elevated trains."

"Maybe I'm the one who's clairvoyant," I said, leading us toward the exit.

"Maybe!" Beth Ann said. "Can you wait while I run this to the room?"

"Sure," I said, "but do you really want to take the chance— leaving it unattended and all that?"

"I guess not," she said, thinking about it without seeming to think about it.

Beth Ann Raymond was from Omaha, a place she more than once referred to as "metropolitan by Nebraska standards." The assistant principal at a middle school, she confessed several things on the walk to the elevated platform at Randolph and Wabash, and among them how she didn't care about pinball.

"Then why go to a pinball convention?" I asked.

"People my age," she said, excavating her truth.

59

"That's all?"

"Well," she hesitated, "other people always seem interested to know there even is such a thing. It's quirky, I guess. Quirky but safe."

I would have let it go at that—a ham-handed admission that it made her feel interesting. But she wanted to give me more.

"And . . ."

"And?"

"Never mind," she said.

"No, and . . ."

"The pinballers don't judge," she said. "Church groups judge. God, do they. But not the pinballers. Short, fat, big, tall, black, white, old, young. I don't think I've ever heard a mean thing said about anybody."

"That's astonishing," I said.

"It is astonishing," she said.

We had been walking under the wooden elevated tracks and soon arrived at the platform's stairs—two tall flights beneath a catwalk. Topside, Beth Ann was winded from the climb, and she seemed to welcome a chance to catch her breath while I explained how to buy a single-ride pass from the Chicago Transit Authority's vending machines.

"My phone!" she gasped, replacing her wallet in the bulky purse. When she did, I glimpsed wads of cash.

"Did you lose it?" I asked.

"No, no, it's in the room! I didn't want to lose my contacts in case something should happen to the money."

"It's fine," I said. "I've got mine."

"Oh, thank God. I'm sorry, Nathan. You must think I'm a head case. But is it a good idea to walk around out here at night? And with no phone?"

"It's barely midnight," I said. "But you can head back if you want. I mean, it's just three blocks that way." I made no indication of the direction.

"Aren't you coming?"

"I will later," I said. "But we just bought tickets. Nothing's going to happen while we're together on the train. We look like a couple. And besides, like I said, I've got my phone."

"Of course. It's fine," she said. "And I still need to say I rode the el."

"Once around the Loop, then I'll buy you a drink at the hotel. Now, which line should we take? The pink, orange, brown, or green?"

"The *safest* one," Beth Ann said, wanting to seem clever.

"The green line it is."

"Is that the safe one?"

"Since when doesn't green mean safe?"

It was ten past twelve when we boarded the second-to-last car of a green-line train to Ashland and Sixty-Third. A group of six heavily inked Latino boys stood huddled and speaking Spanish near the front of the car. Two black girls, who appeared to have just gotten off work at the State Street Target, boarded after us and sat four rows behind. As far as I could tell, there was no one in either the car directly ahead of or directly behind ours. Beth Ann, whether she realized it or not, couldn't have been clutching the top of her purse more tightly. A tone sounded and an automated voice said, "Doors closing."

We sailed south through the Loop, tunneling between tall and mostly darkened buildings. "This is Adams and Wabash," the voice said. We rumbled on in silence, except for the Spanish. "This is Roosevelt. Doors open on the left at Roosevelt."

"Is everything OK?" I asked. Beth Ann's expression was doubtful, her face turning pink.

"It's just that . . . this isn't the view I imagined."

"The Loop's a business district," I said, "and it is Saturday night, after all. Once we get away from the city—"

"Away from the city?"

"Out from underneath all the tall buildings. Then you can take in the skyline for what it's worth." Beth Ann didn't seem encouraged by this. "Do you know where else you can get a great view of the skyline?" I asked.

"No," she said. "Where's that?"

"The lake."

"This is Cermak–McCormick Place," the voice said. "Thirty-Fifth and Bronzeville is next. Doors open on the left at Thirty-Fifth and Bronzeville."

"Nathan, not to spoil the party, but can we head back?"

"Of course," I said. "We just have to get off and wait for a train going the other way."

"How long will that take?"

"Awhile," I said. "Probably this one when it makes the return trip."

"Oh—let's stay put then," she said, full of certainty. She was clutching her chest through the bag.

"This is Thirty-Fifth and Bronzeville. Doors closing."

As the train broke west, away from the Loop, the skyline became visible in distinct pillars of light.

"Now that's more like it," Beth Ann said, admiring the ever-widening view of things.

"This is Forty-Third. Doors closing."

"This is Forty-Seventh. Doors closing."

At the next stop, Fifty-First, four of the six Latino boys got off. At Garfield, the remaining two did. Both girls, who had been sleeping, seemed magically to wake up on the much longer stretch between Garfield and Halsted. When they saw us seeing them, they looked like they wanted to say something. They exited at Halsted. I reached for my phone, which I held low, between my legs, to order an Uber.

"Nathan," Beth Ann said, no longer concealing her worry, "what are you doing? Are we the last ones on this train?" Her neck and cheeks had broken out in irregular, purple blotches. Her breathing was almost as labored as when we had first arrived on the platform—way back at Randolph and Wabash.

"Checking the time," I said.

"What time is it?"

"Twelve forty-five."

"Nathan," she said, squinting through the scored glass, "I can't see the city!"

"Sure you can," I said, finishing with my phone. "It's that way."

"Which way? I can't see anything!" And it was true. From the windows on both sides, the view was a sooty landscape of abandoned buildings, row houses, and trashcan fires.

"Ashland and Sixty-Third is next, this train's final stop. Everyone must exit the train at Ashland and Sixty-Third."

"What?"

"Um, I've got bad news."

"Oh my God! Oh my God!"

"Just listen," I said. "As it turns out, this is the last train of the night. We're going to have to find another way back."

"Oh my God!"

As the train jimmied to a stop, I helped Beth Ann to her feet. "This is Ashland and Sixty-Third, this train's final stop. Everyone must exit the train." The doors opened, but this time they stayed open.

"My age," she murmured.

"What's that?"

"I just celebrated my sixty-third birthday," she said, willing to bargain her pride in exchange for better luck.

"We have to get off," I said, prodding Beth Ann into the stale night air. Behind her, I checked my phone and the driver's progress. "Down these stairs," I said, guiding her with the care a son might offer his mother. "Sixty-three, huh?" I said.

No sooner had we arrived at the bottom of the stairs than in the distance five unevenly spaced shots rang out. Beth Ann flinched with each one but didn't make a sound.

"I'm scared, Nathan," she whispered. "I don't know what to do."

"Let's head this way," I said, "away from the tracks. Toward Marquette."

"Shouldn't we stay on the main road?"

"No," I said. "We'll duck over to Paulina and keep out of sight."

Paulina was more of an alley than a street. Poorly lit and canopied by trees and weeds on both sides, it narrowed sharply as we approached to pass beneath a caged-in viaduct. I walked fast, as if escaping danger rather than leading us to it. Beth Ann could hardly keep up.

"You know all about me," she said, "but I don't know anything about you!"

"Hush!" I said. "Lower your voice." We were hemmed in by a silence as large and dark and yet equally alive as an ocean. The driver was still two minutes away.

"Toward Marquette," she said.

"Yes," I said.

"Wait . . . you're from New York—or so you say!"

"I said I'm from Chicago but I've lived in New York since college."

A car turned north up Paulina from Marquette. I paused, checked my phone, then held up both hands, waving until the driver stopped alongside me.

"How much money is in that bag?" I asked. "You never said."

"Over three thousand dollars!" Beth Ann cried out. "It may be more!" She held the bag out to me with both hands, measuring a space between us I knew she wished weren't there. It was like she was begging me to take it—something I had no intention of doing—to relieve her of the burden of her responsibility, now a target on her back.

"That's a lot of money."

"It may be more!" she said, spending whatever hope was left.

"Since it's my last chance," I said, narrowly opening the car's back door before sliding inside, "I should tell you my name's not Nathan. It's Nick." She heard this with the reaction of one who had not received any worse news in sixty-three years of life.

As the driver sped off, I glanced back just in time to see Beth Ann Raymond, her face as dark and red as the flowers on her bag, dissolving like a spot of blood upon the surface of a black, black sea.

The Phantom Sound of Tones Not There

JACK MCKINNEY WAS BUOYANT with the news: he had been misdiagnosed. A doctor had come to his home to tell him.

"Doctors used to come to you all the time," he once boasted to his grandchildren, soon after his family moved him into the Alzheimer's wing of Bay Tree Estates' sprawling campus. "They'd come see you and give you your news—good or bad. Not like now, when they make you come to them. They get you on *their* turf to tell you how you're finished," he'd said. "They plot you on their charts and even on their phones. Anything to avoid looking you in the eye. It's like you're already dead."

The kids, whose good behavior had been bought and sold on the promise of ice cream, knew to keep their phones out of sight and their attentions fixed on gran-diddy. This is what Emma and Toby, eight and seven, called their father's father, who wasn't sure he liked the name. "But you're the cool grandpa," they said. This he did like, even though their mother's father had been dead for years.

When their father decided the kids had heard enough about doctors as the harbingers of death, he interrupted. "Dad," he said. "I'll bet the kids are ready for some ice cream." *We are!* said their faces.

"Not before Emma shows me how to do Facebook," Jack said. Unlike the lesson on house calls, a Facebook tutorial had been promised, and whatever else did or did not happen, including ice cream, it was Jack's ace-in-the-hole to extend a family visit. From across the room, the children's mother breathed a tired sigh.

"Does that mean I can use my phone now?" Toby asked.

"Sure you can," Jack said. He hoisted Emma to his lap.

"You have a Gateway," she said.

"Is that good?"

"It's old."

"Not as old as I am," Jack said.

"That's true," the girl said. "Do you have an email account?"

"I don't think so."

"If you don't think so then you don't," she said. "But we can set one up."

And the children's mother sighed again.

Jack guessed there had been some debate between his son and daughter-in-law over whether or not it was wise for him to be on Facebook. Six months after joining social media he had amassed 1,727 friends, and his adult family sat him down.

"We think it's great you're online," his son said.

"And that you're a global citizen," Jan added.

"I'm an *American* citizen," Jack said. He was indignant that they had shown up with an agenda but without grandkids.

"That's not what I meant," Jan said. "But you've friended hundreds of strangers in dozens of countries."

This talking-to had the trappings of an intervention. As with the gran-diddy moniker, which for Christmas they had had put on a mug, their exact meaning was unclear. All four of them said "gran-diddy" too often for there not be a joke in it, some secret metonymy against which he could not defend.

"We just don't want you to get scammed," his son said.

What a fine kettle of fish, Jack thought, that at seventy he might be denied what every ten-year-old freely has. This wasn't fair, and yet Jack didn't know how to say it without sounding like a ten-year-old.

"And is it a good idea—" Jan said.

Jack bristled.

"Is it a good idea," his son said, "to have the Alzheimer's ribbon on your profile picture?"

"The kids can change it if it bothers you," he said.

"It's not that," his son said. "But it gives away information about you."

"Your privacy," Jan said.

"I'm not ashamed."

"Nor should you be," she said.

Jack knew how to end the agony. "I see your point," he said. "How about I think about it, then maybe take it down the next time you bring the kids?"

Now, in light of his salvation, everything was turned on its head. Jack was so excited by the doctor's news he decided to go for a walk. He would go alone, even if it was against the rules.

Outside, the sun pressed on the back of his neck like a hot, wet towel. He made slow progress along the shoulder of the highway, where cars and trucks zoomed by. Some drifted past the center line to give him a wider birth and some did not, but all blessed him with a gust of air. Going for walks was a fine idea. There was no chance of getting lost if he went in a straight line along the highway, Jack reasoned, feeling full of himself, and of the day, and of the prospect of the days to come.

Dr. Delany had been to see him that morning. They'd chatted for a long time and not just about Alzheimer's but about grandchildren and the weather.

"I have my doubts," Dr. Delany said, "after talking to you at length like this." He left but soon returned with a device like Jan's phone, only bigger. A house call with a same-day follow-up.

"I have my doubts," he said again, showing Jack some games. "I know these may seem silly, but they're diagnostic. They measure cognition, reaction time, and memory." In one of them, the challenge was to arrange a list of names in alphabetical order by their final letter. In another, the object was to reunite a baby elephant with its mother by prompting it to cross a river using logs labeled with positive words. Helpfulness. Glad. Nice. Love. Home.

Bludgeoned by the sun, Jack turned back. He would be sure to drop a few pounds going for these kinds of walks, he thought. He wondered if, at seventy, he was too old to date. He didn't think so, although his son and Jan would disagree. And what to tell them about this? It was a double-edged sword: if he confessed to being as well as he now knew he was, would they visit more often or less?

"Alzheimer's is shockingly misdiagnosed," Dr. Delany had said before he left the second time. "Over-diagnosed, in my opinion." At the end of the tests, he showed Jack his scores as a percentile of others in his age group. "Unless fifty percent of seventy-year-olds have Alzheimer's, I'd say you're as sharp as a man half your age."

Jack felt pity and a bit of guilt to walk by the reception desk, where other residents' families were signing in. Even though they were strangers, he wanted to tell them his news, but there was no way to do it without sounding like he was bragging.

As he walked in the door of his apartment, Jack was snapped to attention by a blast of cold air. For a moment, he had the dreadful feeling of being in a place he didn't know, of having walked into someone else's home by mistake. Then, with considerable relief, he understood why. It would be someone else's home soon enough. Doubtless he would be moving, he thought, since there was no longer the need to stay here.

In the lap of his recliner was a scrap of paper on which had been written the word "erroneous." Jack remembered asking Dr. Delany to write the word down, since he probably wouldn't recall it—and what better proof of his misdiagnosis than to know what he would forget before he forgot it.

But the questions remained: who to tell and how?

Eventually, Jack settled in at the Gateway to broadcast his news. On Facebook, Emma had made it so the computer remembered his password. "Is that because I'm sick?" he had been brave enough to ask. "No," she said. "Everyone does it that way."

Jack wrote:

> Dear friends, I have exciting news. I have learned my Alzheimer's was misdiagnosed. I have been tested, and a doctor says the diagnosis was erroneous and it happens more often than you would think. Naturally, I am thrilled.

He added a line about looking forward to seeing more of his family, but then took that part out. They would read the post, like everyone else, and could respond accordingly. And when they did, he plotted, he would tell them to bring Emma and Toby so they could remove the purple ribbon from his picture once and for all.

It was midafternoon and Jack, who had not had lunch, made a ham sandwich before watching several episodes of *The Rifleman* and falling asleep in his chair. When he woke up and checked Facebook, the screen swam with hearts. Below the post had come congratulations from all around: "That's WONDERFUL!" "How fantastic, Jack!" "Doctors . . . I'm not surprised." "Bravo!" His grandchildren, too, sent hearts. There were so many comments he couldn't possibly respond to them all, but near the bottom was one he would answer, from Quin Sun, in Tokyo, who had replied, "How did this wonderful thing happen?"

Jack wrote:

> A doctor came to visit today. Like me, he has grandchildren. He recently moved into my wing and says he has years of experience with Alzheimer's. We had a long talk and he performed tests. He showed me my scores and said that the diagnosis was erroneous.

Following this, the comments tapered off but the hearts kept coming. Jack was getting ready to turn in when his son called to ask how he felt about a visit tomorrow. "We'll bring the kids," he said.

"Did you see my news?"

"We did."

Before bed, Jack switched off his computer, grateful to be seeing the purple ribbon for nearly the last time. He drifted to sleep with a joy as familiar to his being as to his sense of being well. But the rest, too, was familiar, and hauntingly so—a vast emptiness to the space he held; a crust, like ice, obscuring words he could no longer see clearly enough to use; and the phantom sound of tones not there.

The War at Home

SARAH HAD NO ILLUSIONS about how to rear a child. (Yes, she even knew one rears, not raises a child—that chickens are raised, or buildings, or funds, but not children.) After the doctors told her she would not likely become pregnant, she leaned on faith. When prayer didn't work, Sarah tried various fertility treatments before going another way.

She and her husband, Emerson, started off fostering kids. In five years, there had been three: Colby, age two, born to a mother on meth; Dustin, age six, whose mother was in prison for selling drugs; and Nichole, also six, whose mother was homeless and could not afford her. Only Nichole's mother seemed to have known from the start that her baby would be taken away and so, according to the caseworker, had given her a white name, perhaps because she thought it would improve her odds. As far as Sarah was concerned, the lesson was never to underestimate a mother's savvy when it comes to protecting her child.

Opposite the ever-changing scene at home, Emerson's work life was so strictly by the book that Sarah wondered if the genes that govern things like intuition weren't altogether absent in him. He was career military, an inventory-supply sergeant in charge of readying divisions for deployment overseas. From boots to bombs, if it did not breathe and could be counted it was his responsibility. Emerson's was a predictable existence, until rumors began to circulate that he too might deploy.

"Word came down I might ship out," he would announce at dinner.

"When?" Sarah would ask.

"Six weeks."

Then, for one reason or another, it didn't happen. Reserves would get the call, tours would be extended, divisions or whole brigades would get shuffled around, and in the end Emerson stayed behind to wield the mighty pen.

Every time "word came down," it sounded to Sarah like a divine edict. Down from where, she wondered. There's an added burden of faith that falls on the shoulders of a soldier's wife, yet no clearer distinction between God and government than when higher-ups change their minds—the infallible versus the flawed, the beatific versus the bureaucratic. Given her druthers, Sarah never would have wished for deployment and, besides, such an outcome would mean the postponement of her own mission: the adoption of a child.

At twenty-eight years old, Emerson had already served abroad—two years in Austria after basic training. Sometimes, he would refer to potential deployment as "going back." That was until Sarah told him not to.

"It's not the same thing," she said.

"Over there is over there."

"When you say you're going back, it implies you've already done a tour in Iraq or Afghanistan." She eased up, without adding that compared to the Middle East his time in Austria sounded like a vacation. "Just don't say going back. It's misleading, even if you don't mean for it to be."

Sarah was kinder to Emerson when he was not around, putting on the requisite fret and especially in front of other military wives. The spouses of those overseas are in a special class, while the wives of those not yet deployed are of lesser rank. For his part, Emerson did not show strong feelings about deployment either way, and word that he would not be going always meant a return to the topic of adoption.

"The next time you're deferred," Sarah said, "I'm calling the agency. Do you want this, Emerson? Because they can tell you don't want it even when you say you do. They're trained to know."

"Of course I want it."

They were on a walk through the woods around Camp Leopold, fifteen square miles of Wisconsin wilderness that this late in the fall was barren and sketched with new snow. For the past few years, talk of adoption had ramped up around the holidays.

"It's just that you seem indifferent about things," she said. "I know it's your nature. I think it makes you seem confident. But the agent won't know you like I do." Flurries began to drift through the web-work of branches. "Of course the burden's mostly on me. In case you should ship out, all parties need to see I can do it on my own." They climbed a steep hill, and the snow began to mix with pellets of ice. "That is until you come back."

"And especially if I don't."

"Don't say that."

"I'm just saying—"

"Don't."

At the top, where they ought to have been able to see right around, clouds came in so low and fast that Sarah wasn't even able to make out the base three miles away. Only a pair of crosses atop the twin spires of St. Anthony's in Warrenville was visible, which to Sarah looked like headstones fixed in the sky. From here, her attention was drawn to a ravine thirty feet below and a culvert bored into the opposing landscape.

"I'm only saying what any agent will be thinking," Emerson said. "The worst can happen."

"I guess," Sarah said, leading the way down the embankment. "Contingency plans aren't always pleasant."

"Are they ever?" he asked.

"Not the kind you're talking about."

At twenty-six years old, Sarah had long been eager to share in the small triumphs and tragedies of parenting. She'd checked out books from the base library, read them, and made Emerson read them: *The Age of Adoption, Once Upon a Child, An Abundant Home,* and others. Sarah took from the books what seemed right and rejected what did not, just as she had taken and rejected wisdom from her mother. Each generation of parents ought to be better prepared than the previous one—and especially adoptive parents, who have the luxury to plan and plan.

Based on the books, Sarah would introduce her child to the church but let him make his own acquaintance with God. She would indulge childhood myths of Santa Claus and a tooth fairy but only until innocence become its own liability, and she would, when the time was right, be forthcoming about the adoption.

Based on her upbringing, Sarah would shower the child with love, and in the years to come she would be at home for him when he returned from school. She would socialize him with other children.

It was the thing Sarah most appreciated about Emerson, that he did not try to get in the way of her plans and priorities, until she began to wonder if he simply did not care.

"I want a son," he said once. "Do we choose that?"

"We do."

"Is a boy all right?" he asked.

"I'd be proud to be the mother of your son."

In early December, word came down that Emerson would be deployed with the second and fifth battalions; but by the middle of January, plans had changed. Only the fifth would go, with a regiment from Camp Lejeune, and so Sarah called the agency.

"Our interview is in March," she told him.

"When do we take delivery?"

"There'll be paperwork, but we should be parents by Easter."

They were walking to the woods again, past holiday displays that continued to disfigure the otherwise orderly tracts of base housing, where each family was in contest with its neighbor to see which could confect a greater joy. By night, small lawns became carnivals of electric snowmen, penguins, reindeer, and other inflatables, lit from below or trussed in LEDs. By day, only hard-plastic Santas remained erect, where around them the frosted plots resembled killing fields of collapsed balloons. The base commander had ordered all such displays taken down by the end of the month.

"I've arranged for a christening during Holy Week, but we need to talk about a name," Sarah said. "The agency is calling him Baby William, but we can do better. I've read books on this. Nothing too generational. No Franks or Ralphs or anything like that."

"What about your father's name?"

"Earl? Are you kidding?"

As they approached the last row of homes, a German shepherd trotted to the edge of its yard, hunched over, and expelled an enormous shit that stood steaming atop spikes of frozen grass.

"How about Rex?" Emerson asked.

"A dog's name?"

"Colter?"

"Too trendy," Sarah said.

"Gunner?"

"Too ridiculous."

"Luke?"

"Too biblical," she said at first. "But we'll keep that one in the hopper."

"Well," Emerson said, "since I picked the gender, why don't you pick the name."

As they passed the last house on the block, the severed head of a ten-point buck gazed up at them from the bottom of a plastic tub. A tarp, put there to protect the owner's trophy from the snow, had blown off during the night and clung to the grill of a nearby truck.

"Imagine," Sarah said. "A year from now we will have celebrated Christmas as a family." But she guessed Emerson was already imaging something along these lines—dreaming, perhaps, of what it would be like, one day, to take his boy hunting.

Emerson met his son, Billy, twice. The first time was on April 3rd, when the agency delivered him. Not that they were expecting a stork—but a Prius? A woman named Denise carried the bundle up the porch steps, her pea-green car, like an alien pod, idling at the end of the drive.

The six-week-old was a gorgeous boy: diamond-blue eyes and already with locks of thick, yellow hair.

"What else can you tell us about the parents?" Sarah asked, offering arms.

"You mean the birth parents?"

"Yes."

"Owing to privacy laws, not much more than I already have. They were both in high school," she allowed, covering part of the child's face with his blanket. "Smart. Healthy." The agent gave the assessment in an officious way that, to Sarah, seemed to hint at some reserved judgment about teens who have babies. "Adoption is such a blessing," she continued. "Neither birth parent has any history of medical problems—other than the father's asthma, which I mentioned before."

"Oh, yes," Sarah said. "Emerson has that."

"Everything else is in the folder. We'll check back in three weeks and again after six months. Otherwise—"

But the couple said nothing. It was the awestruck silence of new parents, taken with their new baby.

The second time father and son met came after Emerson's tour, when Billy could no longer be called a toddler. At three and a half years old, he was all boy. Gone was the amorphous ball of fat his mother had made of him those first eighteen months. Sarah had read that babies who are not fed all they can handle are more likely to develop eating disorders as adolescents and, as a result, by the time Emerson finally did ship out, his son had become quite the chub.

As the tour wore on, however, the child's metabolism came to his rescue and it was Sarah who put on weight—first five pounds and then fifteen. There was nothing but support from other base wives, when a group of women, some with children and some without, met to play bridge on Thursdays.

"Don't worry about it," insisted Mallory Bishé, who gained and lost weight in dramatic swings relative to her husband's deployments. "If you have to, crash diet six weeks before Emerson gets back. We owe them that. 'Til then, who's going to blame us?" Six weeks, Sarah thought. It was already too late. "Besides, you look fine."

"You know," Stephanie Lloyd said, pondering her hand, "my grandmother told me that during World War II, girlfriends and even wives would turn a blind eye to their men's indiscretions. While they were away. Bid."

"Pass. My mother said the same about Vietnam," Jordan Beechner added.

"It's wartime," Meagan Richter said. "Pass. Things are different in wartime."

"Raise. I wouldn't stand for it," Sarah said. "Wartime or not. From my husband? The father of my child?"

Two of the women put down their cards and excused themselves—Meagan to refresh the snack bowl and Alexa to check on the kids.

"Pass. Times are different," Katie said, agreeing with Sarah. "War is different."

"I saw on the news how our pilots in California fly predator drones and can launch missiles from eight thousand miles away," Mallory said.

"Just look at the rest of the country. You'd hardly know we're at war if it weren't on the news." Louise Hawkins, who had twenty years on the next oldest in the group, was the authority on how things used to be. Her husband was General George M. Hawkins, second-in-command at Camp Leopold. "Wouldn't it be something now," she said, "if there's no war after all? If it's a hoax and those men are in the tropics? Cabanas!" She chortled.

"And the women?" Sarah asked.

"Pardon me?"

"The women who serve. Where are they?"

"That's the other difference," Louise said. "Like Mallory says. Women at war. I'll never understand it."

"Maybe they're working the tiki bars," Sarah muttered.

"Pardon me?"

"Here come the kids!" Alexa said, leading a daisy chain of children from the basement, where they had been face painting. She brought them up, through the kitchen, and one at a time into the living room. "Brigitte—the cat!" Alexa proclaimed, and everyone clapped. Everyone except Louise Hawkins, whose fingers touched her lips. "Emma—the clown! Sam—the lion!"

"Precious," Louise let go. "My stars, how precious!"

"Amy—the zebra!"

"I'm a penguin," Amy snapped.

"And Billy—the—" Alexa turned back to the kitchen, where Sarah's boy had been. "Billy?" she called, and Sarah readied herself. "Billy?" Alexa returned to the kitchen. "He must have gone back downstairs," she said on her way to investigate.

"I'm in here," came a small voice from the adjacent bathroom. The door opened and the boy appeared, his face perfunctorily washed, but with smudges of black and blue still staining the skin around his eyes and jaw. "I used to be an elephant."

As annoyed as Sarah had been at the prospect of her son covered in paint, it bothered her as much that he had not wanted to participate in the show.

"Why did you wash it off, sweetie?" she asked on the way home. "Didn't you want to do what the other kids were doing?"

"No," the boy answered. "I mean—yes, I did, but I didn't want paint on my face. I want Daddy to know who I am when he comes home."

"Oh, that's sweet, Billy. But you know your daddy would recognize us no matter what," she said, tweaking her posture and adjusting the lap belt over her stomach.

"No matter what?"

"No matter what."

The troops were to return in cargo planes, a pair of C-17s, which left Kabul at twenty-one hundred hours and were due to touch down at Irwin Field just after two a.m. The plan had been for loved ones to congregate on the tarmac, where there would

81

be enough room for balloons and homemade signs. But the forecast was for storms, and so by ten p.m. texts and an email blast went out, announcing that the roll call ceremony would take place in Hangar 5. One poster per family, please. No balloons.

Sarah went online and scanned radar returns, zooming in on the front until the screen was a field of red pixels. Already she could hear the rain tapping the window, as if by checking she had brought it on herself.

"Billy," she roused the boy in the dark of his room. "It's time." The child staggered out of his pj's and into clothes his mother had laid out. "Do you have to go potty? It's your last chance, sweetheart."

As she drove to the airstrip, gliding down the same wet-black corridor in a procession of other cars, Sarah congratulated herself. Look at him, she thought. This boy. This chosen boy. He is fit, and healthy, and smart, and proud, and he loves his mother and father—his father, whom for two years he had known only as an image on Daddy-cam.

"You tired, pumpkin?" she asked.

"No, Mommy."

Sarah had spent the same two years steeped in the certainty that, on one front or the other, something terrible would happen. Now, on the cusp of reunion, nothing had.

Inside the hangar she searched the vaulted, steel heights and began to catalogue victories. To her credit, Billy was potty trained and could dress himself. He knew his ABCs and could count to twenty in both English and Spanish. He had been fingerprinted and, every six months, photographed. He had been versed in stranger danger. He could recite his phone number and home address from memory, and he had been schooled to share such information only in emergencies and, even then, just with the police or others in authority.

Halogen bay lights blazed down from the ceiling like small, perfectly ordered suns. Cheers went up as coach buses turned in from the rain, aligning against the north side of the building. Sarah spotted General and Mrs. Hawkins on the dais. The howl of a crowd hundreds deep ramped up as soldiers in their service greens appeared, falling in for final roll call.

From where Sarah stood, the men—and they were men mostly—all looked alike. She scanned faces, wondering if she had missed Emerson getting off the bus, while at the same time indulging in the penultimate moment of reunion. It was something owed to her, she felt, as if now she was entitled to thumb her nose at fate and fear. Sarah misidentified Emerson twice, her small smiles budding then fading as joy wound tighter before she picked him out. And because she spotted him first, there remained to be enjoyed his expression when their eyes would meet—Sarah's chance to witness such bliss in the person of her second self.

"Excuse me," Emerson said, as he waded through the crowd toward his wife, looking past her once and then too far left.

He spotted Billy first and then, as if the child were a kind of marker, Emerson looked to Sarah.

"You're more beautiful than the day I left," he swore, moving to take her in his arms, even as she hoisted the golden boy to be kissed first. "I hardly would have known you."

According to Emerson the chances of redeployment were slim, which Sarah accepted as only a non-zero chance. But eight months after he got home, the administration began to draw down troops, and by then Emerson had become fully reengaged in the business of counting things. For Sarah, it was time spent looking for signs and signals. She had read about PTSD and was ready to spot the symptoms: "difficulty concentrating" (though

Emerson had always been distractible), "difficulty falling or staying asleep." Still, this was the Emerson she knew from before.

"How's the—you know?" Mallory inquired.

"The sex?"

"Yes, that."

"Don't worry," Sarah said. "I'd almost forgotten the word too."

"Ha!"

"Great. Compared to not getting it? Phenomenal."

"Nothing like that and a kid to hold the whole thing together."

"Do you fight?" Katie asked.

"What do you mean?"

"You know. Argue? It seems it's all Justin and I do."

"Sometimes," Sarah said. "The other day we were bickering over whether or not to play along about the Easter Bunny and Santa."

"How so?"

"One of the other kindergarteners told Billy it's a lie, and I was all for being upfront. He's the youngest in his class, after all. I don't want him laughed at."

"Children today are too smart for their own good," Louise said.

"Emerson wouldn't let me tell him," Sarah said. "I let it go, since I was the one who pushed for Billy to start school a year early."

"You made the right call, my dear," Louise said. "The whole world's lined up to take away their innocence. Emerson's fighting on the right side."

"Good to know," Sarah said.

Before there was any sign of trouble, Sarah dropped a ceramic dish that Billy had made for her in school. The design of a peacock, glazed and fired in extremis, lay in pieces across the kitchen floor. The letters P-A-V-O, Latin for peafowl, in shards. "Billy!" she shrieked at the loss of a thing so precious. And like he could have heard.

The boy had been playing in front the yard. "With his trucks," Sarah said over and over, as if this might be useful or prove she had been paying attention.

Thirty minutes into it, Emerson rushed home. Neighbors were called. Police were called. For three hours, every time the doorbell rang Sarah lunged to find an adult on the other side, someone else asking if there had been any word. By seven o'clock there was an Amber Alert. By midnight, officially the next day, Sarah had a nervous breakdown and was rushed to the hospital.

For weeks she drifted around the house in a dull frenzy, a listing madness indistinguishable from the effects of so much Demerol. Each hour was its own grim benchmark—past the moment a friend or stranger would show up with Billy in tow, past the moment they might expect a bid for ransom, past the moment either of them allowed themselves to think, for the first time, he was gone for good.

For Sarah, this notion came in the middle of the night, when she shot bolt upright and shook her husband awake. "The culverts," she cried. They'd combed the woods, but had anyone checked the culverts? Emerson had to drag her, half-dressed, back to bed.

"Tomorrow," he swore. "We'll check tomorrow."

"Every one?"

"Every one," he said, cradling her until the hysteria passed.

The television never called it an abduction, as if it's normal for children at play one minute to vanish the next. By fall, the media had stopped talking about it altogether. The new news was the old news. News of the war.

Sarah grew cold and hard. She went for walks alone through woods that burned with color. She stared across the valley for hours at the twin spires of Saint Anthony's.

When she and Emerson were at home together, they didn't talk much.

"We ought to get away," he suggested quietly.

"Where to?"

"Anywhere far away," he said. "Austria. I don't care. Anywhere." It was not yet Thanksgiving, but already the retail world was shoving Christmas down everyone's throat, and the couple agreed that home was the last place either of them wanted to spend the holidays.

"Austria sounds nice," Sarah murmured.

Then there were things that required no discussion, like whether to decorate the house. The only trace of Christmas was a mall photo of Billy, perched on a droll Santa's knee, a framed image that had sat on the mantle for nearly a year. Sarah looked at it dolefully and felt her faith impeached.

"On second thought, maybe not Austria," Emerson said.

"Why not? Do they have Christmas there too?"

"It's less cheerful, but yes."

"How so?"

"Santa's alter ego. Have you ever heard of Krampus?"

"No."

"He's the bad you can't have the good without," Emerson said, studying his wife, who would not take her eyes from the photo. The rest was too much to tell. Details of a horned incubus who roams streets, lashing children before shoving them into baskets to carry them off. Emerson approached her, to see what she was seeing, and in a moment of terrible revelation snatched the photo from the mantle.

"I don't want to go anywhere there's a Christmas," she said with quiet disdain, "anywhere God pretends to be." But Emerson did not hear this. He was already breaking for the door. "Did you hear me? Where are you—?" she asked. But it was too late. He was already gone, in the car and halfway down the drive.

It was thirty-six hours later when the FBI and troopers from the Wisconsin State Police took him down at a VFW post near Waupaca. Lights from vehicles marked and unmarked muted holiday chasers strung carelessly around the building. With weapons drawn on him from every angle, all the man said, as they pinned him to the floor, was that he was a veteran, sixty-two, diabetic. Hauled to his feet, he began to recite a series of numbers. "Three five three seven four one four two. Three five three seven four one four two."

"His army serial number," the agent said. "Are you sure you want to hear this?"

"I do," Emerson said.

"There may be a dozen or more. In and around his home in Ohio."

"How do you know?"

"He kept lists. Names. Home addresses."

"How else would Santa deliver gifts," Emerson said.

"Are you sure you want to hear this?"

He drove through the night. By the time he approached Camp Leopold, it was still dark, and he realized he had not slept in three days. News of the arrest had not broken, but it was coming, soon, he knew. It was enough to have heard about it and then to have identified the child, but now to tell Sarah seemed more than he could bear. Emerson knew it was his duty. And yet what kind of service was this?

Just before dawn, he turned up their street amid the scintillant glow of festival lights. Emerson stopped the car a block from home. He opened the door and leaned out to be sick on the curb. Inside, his wife was awake and standing not far from where she had been when he left.

"For God's sake where have you been?" Sarah would have scolded him more had she not been so afraid. Emerson looked like a madman coming at her, taking her by both arms and pressing her to the wall, like he was about to offer violence.

Because, in a way, he was.

Part Two

The Crab

THEY HANDLE DEATH DIFFERENTLY in the South—soften it up with slow speech or shoo it like a horsefly threatening to sting, which is not to say this is better or worse than how they cope in other places, just that it's different.

But it's summertime, when death is not much on anyone's mind and horseflies are a legitimate nuisance, and Mattie is eager to run down to the marsh to play with the other girls, Shell and Iris. There's a long wooden pier that angles like a broken leg one hundred yards through mud and tall grass to a river that doesn't flow so much as it rises and falls with tides. The marsh is more fun for the girls than the shallow pools of water between houses or tracts of undeveloped woodland, where the only living creatures are ants, songbirds, and snakes. In the marsh, there is an assortment of life: rabbits, strange white birds that look like they've been folded out of paper, small dark hens, gators, and crabs—both fiddler and blue.

Except for Mrs. Dismuke, who is said to feed loaves of white bread daily to a large gator that comes to sun in her backyard, Ruthie has neither seen one nor heard of anyone seeing one, and Ruthie has lived by the water all her life. Gator sightings, as she understands it, are the purview of those with backyard swimming pools or small dogs. In her mind, the danger is the dock itself. It is in poor repair—rickety, rotting beneath, and missing planks (and that had been its condition years ago, the last time she had been on the dock).

"You *walk* to the end!" Ruthie hollers from the belly of a recliner, where she is stranded by her weight. "Don't run!" Ruthie doesn't have to guess—she knows where her granddaughter is

91

going. To Mattie, her grandmother is Mee-Maw and always will be.

But the girl is already running, a jellied mass of chicken gizzards, necks, and backs spotting a pink trail from one corner of a Butternut Bread bag. Mattie brings the bait, Shell the traps, and Iris just herself. This is how it works. Although she didn't ask if she could have the chicken, Mattie can't imagine Mee-Maw will object, especially when she comes home with a cooler full of crabs for supper. Mattie imagines herself in this way—larger than life, like some kind of hero.

The midday heat is archetypal, the bayou's best impression of hell where white light squints the eyes from a sky so full of sun that the only relief is to keep one's gaze to the ground. By nine thirty, Mattie and Iris are standing at the cusp of lawn and marsh with the Devonshire estate to their backs.

"You got the traps?" Mattie asks. The blood soup has drained away and only flaps of yellow fat and violet bone remain, which she displays to suggest they need a trap more than they need Shell. Even as she asks, Mattie knows Iris will say "No ma'am." Iris is black and poor—poor like Mattie, but somehow, and in ways she can't explain, it's better to be white and poor than black and poor.

Mattie would never say "No ma'am" to Iris.

"We gots to have a trap?" Iris asks.

"Yeah, dummy!"

But they don't have twine either. Shell is supposed to bring that, too, so Iris says nothing and sits beside Mattie on an oyster bed, and they wait.

Without saying anything, Ruthie curses Tom for skipping work. They can't afford indulgences, and although she stops short of calling it an indulgence to attend a funeral, the result is the same.

"I was the only white person there," Tom says. "Sat in back." These were as many words as he had said to his wife in days.

"Was there many people?"

"Yep."

Ruthie moves her head as a prelude to getting up, which is not going to happen.

"One of 'em, I think it was the sister, throw'd herself on the body whilst the casket was still open," Tom says. Ruthie does not want to interrupt, lest the miraculous speech stop.

"That right?"

"It was quite a show." Tom opens a can of beer. "I have to say, it weren't what I expected. That's the thing about death. You don't get what you expect."

Ruthie wouldn't have moved even if she could have. Struck by this odd, philosophical brush, she wonders if Tom stopped for a beer at Twin Oaks on his way home or if this man is some kind of imposter. If he keeps on like this, Ruthie decides she'll refrain from mentioning he can still earn a half-day's pay if he goes to work.

"What'd she die of?"

"Cancer," Tom says, downing half the can.

"The crab," his wife murmurs.

"Stomach."

Ruthie shudders to hear this. She cannot explain why, but ever since she was a girl she has been sure that this would be her fate. Every occurrence in another person, known or not, terminal or not, is a harbinger of her own death.

"It was good of you to go," she says. "She reared you and your sister, after all. Even if she did get paid. God knows I ain't gettin' paid to bring up this one." Ruthie is thinking of her granddaughter, robbing the marsh and the neighbors of their lot.

"Where's she at?" Tom asks.

"Crabbin'," Ruthie says.

"Again? There won't be a crab left in Terrebonne Parish by the time school starts." Tom sits up and leans forward. "She ain't at the Devonshire place is she?"

"Didn't say she wasn't."

"Damn. I hate that," he says. "What if they come back and decide to use their dock and them girls is down there? Anything wrong'll be our fault."

"Easy to blame the poor," Ruthie says absently, her fingers twitching as she spots the remote, which has fallen to the floor.

"I'm goin' to work," he says, swilling the rest of the beer.

"Drunk?" Ruthie says. Although she regrets such discouragement, Tom is not fazed. On the way out, he bends over, retrieves the remote, and places it on the TV tray near his wife, as one would furnish a dog with its bone. She had not asked for it and yet is grateful.

Their bodies are like jewels fresh from the mine, but better than jewels because they move. Metallic-blue backs with bright cayenne claws dotted in pearl teeth, the promise of a pinch worse than the reality. Even though Shell brings the traps, Mattie insists on being the one to hoist them to the surface. It's her bait, she reminds the others. And, besides, this is her spot.

It's a magical moment to draw the weight against the resistance of dark water, when the O-framed basket clears the surface and there's a crab or two or three leeching to the bait. Iris is appointed to overturn the traps into the cooler. If someone is going to get pinched, it's probably going to happen during this transfer. Occasionally, one will fall short and launch itself from the end of the dock into the safety of the river. When this happens, it's convenient to blame Iris and subtract the loss from her total.

The afternoon can pass slowly on a dock. As the tide rises, the prospect for more crabs dims. Low tide gives the best luck, and the girls are aware of how shallow the river is when the waterline has receded the full six feet from the platform, exposing mounds of soft mud on both sides of a ford that's plugged with marsh grass and pocked with holes bored by fiddler crabs.

"I gots t' pee," Shell proclaims before disappearing to the shore. When she returns, trotting down the planks, she's cradling a rock.

Iris spots her first, wobbling toward the left side of the pier then overcorrecting and nearly falling off the right. She stops short, six inches from the edge, and the missile plummets. It barely clears the end of the dock before plunging through ductile mud and out of sight at the river's edge. There's a wake as water fills the void. Fifteen feet away, two herons loll into a jade sky.

"Way to go, dummy," Mattie snaps. "Way to scare the crabs!"

"What's left of 'em," Iris says.

The fact is, Mattie's last four pulls have come up empty, and most of the bait has been scavenged away.

"Whaddaya care?" Shell says. "'Sides, tide's comin' in."

"But we only got nine!" Mattie feels like crying, but more from rage than disappointment. "Nine ain't enough! That's only five for me and that ain't enough to stuff a snail!" The other girls don't question her math.

"That's okay, cheater," Shell says, turning back down the dock. "You can have mine. I'm tired. I'm goin' home."

"Mee-Maw, I done caught eight!" Mattie screeches, circumnavigating the yard's obstacles: car tires, a bicycle frame, a couch, a box spring, and assorted wheeled toys. Ruthie is on her feet, limping to the door to meet her granddaughter.

"My stars, child. Eight what?" Ruthie already has a five-gallon pot on a burner out back. "Crabs?"

Mattie remembers she forgot to ask permission for the bait—or to go in the first place—and puts on a sad look to augment whatever mercy eight crabs might buy.

"What's y'all gonna eat? I know," Ruthie cajoles. "You and Tom can have the chicken I was savin'." She finds it hard to be angry with the girl. As much as she despises Mattie's mother, her own daughter, Ruthie tries to adore her granddaughter as if she is a kind of second chance. "Let's get a look."

"They's big, Mee-Maw," the child says. When the cooler's lid is removed, there comes an uninspired scuttle toward the top. The crabs are the color of dirt, more bronze than blue. Having been out of the marsh for hours, the color of their claws has turned from pink to brown.

"There's nothin' to 'em," Mee-Maw says. "Put the lid back on. I've got a pot out back. I guess it's enough if I fix cornbread. I swear, child, ya'll have crabbed that marsh to extinction."

At the mention of a pot, Mattie understands that all is right with the world. The cooler feels lighter as she shuffles barefoot over the kitchen's scored linoleum, curling along its seams like parchment. On the back stoop a pot is waiting, wide enough at its base to eclipse the gas burner beneath. The water is at a rolling boil, so furious Mattie cannot see the bottom.

The crabs look like Samurai, with daggers for eyes flitting in and out of russet shells while bubbles of air cluster around their mouths. In the failing daylight, they do seem smaller than they had on the dock, Mattie thinks. Mee-Maw follows her through the kitchen, stopping at the cupboard to bring out some cornmeal and grease.

"Here ya'll go," the girl says, like she's doing the crabs a grand favor, when she tips the cooler and causes them to tumble by their own weight into the pot. Suddenly the water is still. But the crabs are not still. For several seconds, they go insane with trauma.

Ruthie watches her granddaughter from her side of the gnarly screen. It does not bother her that Mattie went crabbing without permission, or that she helped herself to the chicken without asking, or that she might even have been mean to the other girls and bullied them out of their share of the catch. But it bothers her that Mattie is not afraid of this part—the part that should be hardest. Even the boys Ruthie knew growing up shied away at the end. But not Mattie. When the time comes to deal the crabs into the pot, there is no holding her back.

"Mattie, you is Queen of the Crabs," Tom says, wiping his mouth and popping the tab on another beer. The girl's face glows. She loves the attention, loves her grandpa, and invites greater praise.

"Mee-Maw says I crab too much. Says there won't be no crabs left."

Ruthie holds her tongue. It's all she can do not to make it known Tom had said this first. Somehow, Ruthie always comes out on the short end of the stick.

Because it's hot, they sit on the front porch, where patched screens are barely enough to keep them from being eaten alive by mosquitoes. By eight thirty, the sun has set behind their shanty, and the buzz of cicadas from surrounding woods ratchets up. In the space of one beautiful hour, the tops of pines fade from green, to rose, to violet.

"I'll tell ya what we'll do," Tom says, moved by the creative force of the beer. "Gather up all them claws!"

"What claws?"

"The crab claws, silly!"

"They's been throw'd out."

"It don't matter."

"Tom—" Ruthie tries to intercede from the couch, but despite her enormous presence, she has no say and Tom shushes her with a wave of his hand.

"I'll get 'em out the trash! What're we gonna do?"

"We'll clean 'em up, bleach 'em 'til they's white as stars, then we'll make ya a crown with pinchers runnin' all around the outside. You think you'll have enough?"

"Stink up creation," Ruthie wheezes.

"Don't pay her no mind," Tom says. "She's just sore 'cause she can't be Queen."

"Who gets to stay here all day and smell it? Not you. Not Her Highness."

"If there ain't enough, I know where we can get more," the girl shrills, cautious in her exuberance not to mention the Devonshire place by name.

"Lord, if we don't already owe these crabs a heavenly debt." Ruthie is at her wit's end, giving it all she's got to stand.

"Run on," Tom says, "and fetch them claws."

To the west, the wind kicks up. Through the pines comes thunder. For several minutes, neither Tom nor Ruthie speaks. He drinks and she broods. Then, as if on cue, lightning fractures the sky, and the rain starts—first in drops that are easy to count and then in floods of sound like static.

"I don't know why you insist on makin' my life so hard," she says.

"Trouble with you is you don't know how to have no fun." The temperature drops, and all hell breaks loose—hail and a torrent that sprays in waves across the roof.

"And who gets to stay here all day to smell it? Not you. Not Mattie."

"On second thought, I might be wrong," Tom says. Mists of cold rain hiss through the shoddy screens. He stands up, offering a hand to Ruthie. "Maybe you is Queen of the Crabs."

It rains for three days, and Mattie's mood worsens by the hour. "It's only water! Water never killed nobody!"

The girl is a terror, and Ruthie would just as soon get her out of the house as have her there, with the sinister band of claws balanced on her head and a smell like rotten fish trailing behind.

"Prisoner in my own home," Ruthie moans.

"That's 'cause you's so fat," the girl says. She knows Mee-Maw can't chase her.

But Mattie's glory is incomplete—her crown like a smile with teeth missing—and there is only one place to go to complete the mission.

By Tuesday afternoon the rain tapers off, and Mattie calls Shell and tells her to meet her at the dock.

"Can I go now?" Mattie tries one last time.

"No, child! How many times I gotta tell you. It ain't our dock." The girl sees why Mee-Maw is cross: the television remote is on the floor beside her ankle, which is the size and texture of a cantaloupe. Mattie picks up the device and, with deference, places it on the table. It is behavior, the girl concedes, not befitting royalty.

"What do you say?" Mattie asks.

"What I say is if you go to the Devonshire place, I *will* get up out of this chair and I *will* whip the daylights out of you!"

For the half mile that runs from the shanties through woods to the marsh's edge, small kettles of low ground connect in soft pools of water. They make for patterns that skew the once familiar landscape, so it takes Mattie an extra few minutes to arrive at the Devonshire's estate. Around back, she discovers Shell is not there, and Mattie begins to stew. A few minutes later, the sky spoils and the rain resumes.

In all directions the marsh is bloated with the tide and rain. The water level creeps up, licking the good grass at the foot of the yard. Farther out, vast, swirling fields of gray water bury the patches of reed that usually outline tributaries. All is sea. Even without a way to track the time, Mattie decides to wait for Shell. A minute later, she gives up. Her crown's cardboard frame, worse than being incomplete, is waterlogged and slipping from her brow.

Irritated as much with Mee-Maw as Shell, Mattie turns and nearly runs into her friend. Both girls' hair is lacquered to their heads.

"Nice hat," Shell says, trapless and without so much as a ball of twine. The crown slips to the tip of Mattie's nose, then around her neck like a noose. A bag of hearts, the least part of the fowl, sags hopelessly toward the ground.

Thunder drones beyond the horizon, past fetid marsh and out over the gulf. The air is warm, moist, and uncommonly pleasant.

"I came for crabs and I ain't leaving without crabs."

Shell watches as Mattie turns toward the dock, now little more than a footpath.

"I only gotta have *two* more," she yells back.

"You ain't gonna catch nothin'," Shell says, following anyway. The planks are green with mold, and water bobs up between them. Walking is more like balancing on a raft. Reeds litter the way—evidence that the tide has recently been above boards. On both sides of the dock, currents churn in broad eddies.

"You ain't gonna catch nothin'," Shell says again, but Mattie is too far ahead.

At the end of the channel, where the pier widens to a square platform, the river has risen seven feet, distended to the lip of the dock. Mattie has never seen the water so high or fast. The air is thick and cold, and Mattie takes off her crown and puts it at her feet between them.

"What if we can't get back?" Shell asks, but already Mattie is removing her shoes, ready to take a seat and let her legs dangle in the rushing, black water.

"What do you mean?"

"What if the dock washes away?" It's not like Shell to worry, and this makes Mattie bolder.

"I guess we'll be stuck out here. Put your feet in." Shell, adapting to the new role of subject, takes off her shoes. "Or maybe we'll get swept away," Mattie says. "Lots of stuff *could* happen."

Shell dunks her legs into the water, and the current jerks her calves toward the river bend, pulling her fanny forward. "Whoa!" she gasps as her hands slam against the surface. "Or maybe we'll die!"

"Maybe," Mattie says. "But I don't think so."

"Why not?"

"Because I'm Queen of the Crabs." Mattie offers this insight with great humility, onerously, as she reclaims her crown to inspect it for damage. "That's why."

"Who made you queen of anything?"

To the east, beyond where the marsh ends and the gulf begins, a new blackness claims the horizon, broken every few minutes by the faint flicker of a lightning field. It's getting late and, with the weather, hard to tell how long before dark.

"I have an idea," Mattie says, her face as brooding as the sky. She knows she won't get what she came for, and because she is not used to being denied, someone must be punished. Mattie puts on the crown, as if to summon both the courage and the authority it brings. "Here's what I want you to do."

"Mattie's done fell in!" Shell screams with what feels like her last breath. She's run the entire way back, only to find Ruthie on her feet (not what she had been told to expect), frying a skillet of okra for dinner. *"Down at the end,"* she gasps, full of drama, before collapsing onto the floor.

Fifteen years later, Mattie is home for her grandfather's funeral. It's winter, but the Devonshires are not home. A maid answers the door and consents to the young woman going out back, where Mattie is struck by how nothing much has changed. She shudders to be in the same place, under the pergola where she hid as a child, seeing the marsh.

Nothing will ever change.

Color is siphoned from the sky, and from the side of the house Mee-Maw appears as an apparition plodding for the dock. The girl hardly knew her grandmother could walk, let alone run, and by the time Mattie makes it to the end of the yard, Mee-Maw is already halfway down the jetty.

But now Mattie walks slowly, knowing how the vision ends. It's the dream that haunts her in the city, where the crabs are with her always—the great survivor crabs, her subjects, coming back again and again on menus, in cartoons, and on advertisements to remind her who wins in the end.

At the edge of the dock, Mee-Maw would have seen the crown she'd left—but when the young woman arrives, only the jagged teeth of shorn planks remain, now as then, and a long fall to the bank, and the river, and a life abundant, always there just beneath the surface.

A Prayer of Humble Access

Day One—July 2

BEFORE THE CAR CRASH that took his life, the Reverend J. Maurice Ovens refused to travel by plane. It didn't matter that he had had several brushes with death, two cancers and a stroke, flying scared the man, and so he insisted to drive. His wife, Lula, had decided years ago that it was no longer a matter worth arguing over, even if it did cost them an arm and a leg in gas and six full days apart—three on each side of a month-long vacation.

"You could ride with me," he used to offer, but Lula was stubborn, and besides, as she told him, there was something to be said for time alone with one's thoughts.

They had not planned to keep the house on the island after Lula's mother died, but before they knew it, two decades had slipped by and a pattern was set: nine months teaching history at Yeats Middle School in Jasper, Indiana, a month to recover, a month to vacation in South Carolina, and a month to get ready to repeat the cycle.

The annual vacation was equal parts pleasure and pain, not the worst of which was a heat so tropical that even early in the morning it was enough to make Lula's brown skin blush. She no longer recognized people or places. Except for Sparkle Nation, who kept an eye on the house, and Mr. Torregrossa, others she once knew had moved away or died. The character of the island also had changed. As time passed, it had gotten younger. Younger and whiter. Now here she was, a large black woman of late middle age, sitting alone outside the Sand Dollar Café, furtively tossing muffin crumbs to a sparrow the size of her middlemost fingers.

"DO NOT FEED THE BIRDS" signs were common along the boardwalk. It was as if to suggest that the most indigenous of the island's residents were no longer welcome. Lula remembered being a little girl, standing not ten feet from where she now sat, when a gull tagged her on the back of the neck. With no harm done, nobody thought they needed to make a sign then.

Where Maxwell's Dime Store and Roberta's Beauty Shoppe used to be, nightclubs and condos had gone up, and that wasn't the worst of it because now even the change changed. In the space of several years, and in a single location, a tee-shirt shop could become a nightclub, a bookstore, a restaurant, and a tee-shirt shop again. Except for a visit from Mr. Torregrossa, who was ambling toward her through the parking lot, Lula didn't know what to expect from one summer to the next.

"Mrs. Ovens! Is it July already?" he said, inviting himself to sit.

"Mr. Torregrossa, you lookin' good as ever." If he could pretend, then so could she, Lula thought, because the man looked like hell. For someone who lived on the island, Tony Torregrossa was as pale as paste, squat, with a protruding belly that he carried low and wide as if concealing a pillow beneath his shirt. He was never without the same hat, woven from plaited jipijapa. It was like this every summer—Mr. Torregrossa, trolling the village in the days before Maurice was due, to try to talk her into selling the house. For each of the past four years he had made a better offer, but Lula knew his game, and legitimacy was the man's last resort. Once, he had even tried to get the county to declare her house a blight. They sent a letter, as required by law, to inform her that a petition had been filed. When eminent domain failed, he had no choice but to throw money at her.

106

The house had been her parents' parents' and the one in which Lula had grown up—a sturdy, melon-colored Cape Cod, which by virtue of a century's worth of hurricanes and erosion had been promoted to near-beachfront property. On both sides of the home were twin jewels in the Torregrossa real estate crown: a hotel, Palmetto Court, and an equally garish compound in pink stucco, the Island Club Golf & Tennis Resort. For a decade, the only thing standing in the way of connecting these monstrosities was the Ovens' property. Until Mr. Torregrossa tried to take the house by force, Lula and her husband rented it, but fearing he might do something stealthy, like arrange for someone to let the place and then trash it (or worse), she preferred to have it sit empty eleven months of the year.

"How's that husband of yours?" Mr. Torregrossa asked. Every year she imagined he waited to learn that Maurice had died, with the expectation that surely then she would sell.

"He don't fly," Lula said. "Says it ain't God's plan."

"But what about his health? His health is good, ain't it?"

"Maurice's health is fine."

"Well, Mrs. Ovens," said Mr. Torregrossa, "I do wish you'd let me take that house off your hands." A cord of perspiration gathered on his brow. To Lula, Tony seemed troubled, as if he had already begun to assume a share of her burden. He reached into his jacket pocket and produced a card on which was written his latest offer. "Seein' as how you don't have no family here and how expensive it's got to be keepin' the place up." Lula held out her hand, as much to take the card as to let Mr. Torregrossa know she had heard enough.

"I'll have to discuss it with my husband."

"I know," he answered, removing his hat and holding it in one hand. Where the band had been, a rose line marked his forehead.

It was only seven-thirty, but already the sun whirled down in pinwheels of light above the waterfront. Mr. Torregrossa leaned in before standing. "So, I'll see you before you leave?"

This was, as Lula heard it, not so much a question as a threat. "I reckon so," she said.

Lula finished breakfast, now inviting as many birds as she pleased to clean her plate. She didn't need to look at the card to know what a fantastic figure would be there, more than she would make in many lifetimes of teaching sixth grade. Lula had seen such offers before but was wondrously immune. Still, as she walked past the lighthouse and palettes of empty beach, she wondered why she did not sell.

Halfway home, Lula stopped to rest beside the bronze replica of a cannon, and to read the plaque that had been set into its tabby base: 379 British Died Here And South of the Point to Defend the Colony Against The Spanish Advance. Lula was testing the shells that framed the inscription when the lip of an oyster nicked her middle finger—a clean cut, one-quarter inch across and just as deep. Blood spotted the ground as she rummaged her purse for a tissue. Lula wondered if she had peroxide at home or if she ought to go back to the village to buy some. Peroxide keeps, she reasoned, but then changed her mind.

Her thoughts returned to the house. Why didn't she sell—unless for the fact the Italian man wanted so it much? Maurice, as much as he had enjoyed their summer trips, had been indifferent to status or material gain. For him, she recalled, the property and its view were both alien and splendid, his reward for another year of work and something to look forward to on the drive from Indiana.

As the home came into sight, the tide was low and appeared like a broad line on a canvas of sand. Ships, tankers mostly, rested on the sound that was a route to ports between Beaufort and

Savannah. It was an insult like no other, she thought, that the Italian man had suggested her home was an eyesore when it was these buildings of his that disfigured the landscape.

Lula stopped at the foot of her porch to look for blight. For its defects, which were negligible, the house was a gem. Even the strips of paint peeling along the trim added to its character. The house was old, like the island. Blight, she scoffed, more put off than before and passing her gaze from one to the other of the adjacent properties. Her home's only fault was that it made the developments on either side look so much worse.

Inside, Lula found a bottle of peroxide in the first place she looked, and so was glad not to have gone back to spend money on something she didn't need. She dressed her wound. Why not wipe out the whole beach, she thought. Take down the historical monument, too, and build a mile of ugliness from the pier all the way to the north end. There'd be no more blight if it was all blight, she reasoned.

Day Two—July 3

The day before the accident, Maurice had gotten only as far as Louisville and then compounded his sin by not calling.

"I can make it up," he said when he phoned the next day, "once I get to Georgia. There ain't nothin' in Georgia 'cept long, flat roads." It was the last time they had spoken, and the conversation remained fixed in Lula's mind.

"And state troopers, who don't care if you preach the Word or not when you're a black man speedin' through their state."

Now, four years later, as she held the receiver, Lula felt young again—younger, anyhow—and in a way that made her not want to set it down.

"I thought you'd want me there as soon as I can get," she imagined him saying.

"If I'd wanted that, I'd have checked you with the rest of my bags. What I want is you here safe. This house ain't goin' no place," Lula promised. As she waited for Maurice to ask what she meant, someone knocked on the door.

Lula pulled back the valance to see Sparkle Nation standing away from the threshold, the sun rising between her ankles. Sparkle was white, twenty years younger than Lula, and a good Christian.

Lula opened the door, letting in shafts of light. The friends hugged. Sparkle was a large woman but, unlike Lula, she carried most of her weight up high around her shoulders and arms. In her hands was a brick of letters and other bound mail.

"How are you, Mrs. Ovens, after all this time?"

"Don't seem like a year," Lula said, taking the bundle.

"Sometimes a day feels like a year on this island."

"Ain't that right?" Lula said. "And you know I don't sleep."

"Ever?"

"Hardly ever," Lula said. "I'm sorry Maurice ain't here yet." She took the mail and cradled it like a pet. Sparkle had lost her husband years ago, and so Lula was careful with her words. It was, she knew, the kind of loss a person never gets over.

"That man's as slow as the itch," Sparkle said. It was the same every year, a passion play of sorts and, like gathering the mail, Sparkle knew her role. "When's he expected?"

"I hope before that Italian man comes back," Lula said. "C'mon, let's you and me sit out here." The pair moved to the porch and took a seat facing the sea. "I don't mind if he spots me, so long as I've got company."

"If he comes by, he won't stop."

"If he does, I'll just excuse myself."

"May I ask you something, Mrs. Ovens?"

"Umhum."

"It's personal."

"That don't bother me."

"Why don't you sell the place? You could still visit the island whenever you like."

"You're as bad as that man."

"Mr. Torregrossa?"

"You know he's always saying the same thing."

"Maybe he's got a point."

"He ain't got no point. He was all up in my business yesterday talkin' 'bout 'How's Maurice?' and 'How's his health?'"

"I'm sure he doesn't mean any harm. Progress may not always be pretty, but it's inevitable."

"I expect he's waiting for Maurice to kick off, if you wanna know the truth. So I'll give up and sell. Where'd we be if those British had given up?" Lula said, with the monument in mind.

"Pardon me?"

"The British, you know—them three hundred and some all."

"I guess we'd be speaking Spanish," Sparkle joked. "You know what tomorrow is?"

"Independence Day."

"It's Sunday. Maurice won't be here, so why don't you come to church with me?"

"He might be. He says he's gonna speed through Georgia. Besides, why would I wanna go to a white church?"

"Lord, Mrs. Ovens, I ain't askin' you to go to the Episcopal church. There are black folks at First Methodist."

"I guess there ain't no harm in it."

"I guess not either," Sparkle said, standing up. "Then, after supper, I'll come by and we'll drive to the village and watch fireworks."

"I might watch the fireworks with Maurice."

"If he's not here, then. You know Maurice."

"Ain't that right," Lula said.

It was the time of day when the earliest risers from Palmetto Court began to make their way to the shore: skinny white women, some with wide-brim hats and large, black sunglasses. Lula often wondered what they thought of her house, sitting up straight and proud like a tribute to the past.

"Shall I pick you up at ten, Mrs. Ovens?"

"What's that?"

"Ten o'clock? For church?"

"Ten'll be fine."

"One more thing, Mrs. Ovens, while I'm thinking of it." Sparkle stopped and turned on the lowest step, where the wood became sand. "It might be a good idea to get phone service in the house, I mean, if you want it to seem like a bona fide residence. As it is, there ain't no way for me to get in touch with you if somethin' should happen. At least not from here."

Day Three—July 4

There were no black people at First Methodist, and Lula wondered if Sparkle had been mistaken or lied outright, or maybe they had skipped services and were home with their families. She liked this last possibility best, so she stuck with that. Still, she was sorry she went. They might as well have gone to the Episcopal church, Lula thought, with its finery and inaccessible language. She and Maurice had visited years ago, but they'd understood little of the rituals or the rites.

We do not presume to come to this thy Table, O merciful Lord, trusting in our own righteousness, but in thy manifold and great mercies—We are not worthy so much as to gather up the crumbs under thy Table—We have followed too much the devices and desires of our own hearts—We have done those things which we ought not to have done, and there is no health in us.

It was strange for Lula, who had never known white people to grovel, and she was left with the impression Episcopalians must think it permissible to sin freely all week as long as they save up their contrition for Sunday. The island's elderly had traditionally taken refuge at Saint Mark's, where on Lula's visit she'd recognized more than a few specters, each one a widow. They had been old enough then and to her looked like rows of gilded skeletons. If these ghosts and foreign prayers and sad hymns and peculiar smells were not enough to keep her from going back, it was also where the Italian man, Mr. Torregrossa, went to church.

It was noon before the Methodist service ended, and one o'clock by the time Sparkle had exchanged her gossip and gotten Lula home. At least the phone would not be ringing. She could thank Sparkle for reminding her of that and saving her from any chance she might relive the call from the Georgia State Police, telling her of the accident.

Soon after it happened, Lula had taken steps to see to it the phone would never ring again. For four years, Mr. Torregrossa probably thought it was her way of avoiding him, and she was happy to let him think so, even if it was no solution to the larger problem of avoiding him for the rest of the month, just as it had been every July, lest he learn her secret.

Lula made tea and decided to take her chances on the porch. The tide was going out, and soon the shore grew crowded with parti-colored loungers and umbrellas. Before she sat down, she spotted a postcard that had been wedged into the railing, where it split from a vertical beam beside the steps.

113

Lula collapsed into her rocker, cackling like a hen. Mr. Torregrossa must have dropped off the card personally, as it was hand-signed at the bottom: "I hope you and your husband will join us."

This was the same fireworks display she had watched for years—without an invitation—from the porch where she was sitting. Her porch. They might not be the best seats in the house, but for such a humble access it was better than anything she could get at the public display in the village, which reminded Lula she would need to have an excuse ready for Sparkle. She had read in the paper that Mr. Torregrossa spends tens of thousands of dollars, and more each year, to put on the best display in South Carolina. His guests pay through the nose to be there, but for Lula it was free and the one occasion she seemed to be stealing from him and not the other way around.

By eight-thirty, the sun was behind her. The tide out. The dome of sky above the ocean darkened from mauve, to purple, and then to black. Sparkle didn't stay long and seemed to know as soon as she arrived that Lula would beg off. It was part of the ritual, after all, another scene in the play.

First came the irregular crackle and hiss from local artisans, children with their own shows setting off bottle rockets and Roman candles. By nine o'clock, slide whistles split the sky and a succession of booms like cannons sounded on the horizon. The air cooled, as if a squall was gathering, and Lula, from sheer anxiety, began to rock more urgently in the salty breeze.

The first explosions arrived with the muted glow of distress flares. Lula imagined the Spanish Armada, aligned off the coast, back after two centuries to reclaim something they felt was theirs—something worth dying for—and here she was, a widow, without so much as a firearm in the house and with an empty chair beside her to broadcast her solitude.

The attack ramped up, with blooms of light opening in different parts of the sky: red, blue, and green, flash preceding report before fingers of smoke distended over the beach. She could smell the gunpowder like mesquite, the improbably sweet smell of fuel in action. Every year Lula gave a lesson to her sixth graders about Japanese culture and the origin and meaning of fireworks. *Hanabi*, the Japanese call them. Flowers of fire. Like flowers, they bloom and perish sooner than they should.

But flowers in the East are weapons in the West.

Mortars fired in continuous rounds, and the sand before her began to glow, reflecting rainbow colors and exposing troops of people more awestruck than afraid. Streaks of silver smoke clawed apart the sky, opening holes where suddenly the moon revealed a fleet of vessels on the water—so many she couldn't count them all.

The armada, Lula panicked, scurrying to her feet, *and without a defender in sight!* She rushed into the house and out again, keys in hand to lock the door. If they were going to take her, at least they would not take her home.

"Mrs. Ovens, I came to apologize." Mr. Torregrossa was at the bottom of the steps, looking shorter than usual but ever the suppliant, his left hand raised as if praying to be lifted up. "I saw Mrs. Nation in the village and she told me about Maurice. I had no idea! Please, believe me, I wouldn't have brought up your husband all this time, Mrs. Ovens, if I'd known."

Lula was struck dumb by such betrayal, now with the last of her defenses breached. And what a fine outcome this was: that the Italian man couldn't wait until morning to lay claim to what he knew was destined to be his; couldn't wait until his pyrotechnics were over, his gold spent, before rushing to her door to plant a flag.

"I have what you came for, Mr. Torregrossa," Lula said. With her back straight, she lobbed the keys over his head and into the dunes.

"Then I'll have a man over tomorrow, if that's all right, with a contract. For the price offered, of course." Mr. Torregrossa had to yell above the din of his own making, a war-zone of color and spectacle exploding at his back.

"You want me to find your keys, Mrs. Ovens?" he offered, moving to retreat.

"They're your keys now," Lula said.

And she had a point.

Mr. Torregrossa would have thought it wise, while there was still some sort of light to see by, to scavenge the sands and have them when he returned—as a safeguard, if nothing else, against any chance the woman might also forget this, her most recent history.

Hard Time

I

THERE WAS A TIME when having a flat tire was the prologue to adventure: You walked when you'd planned on doing no walking. You engaged people you otherwise would have avoided. You assessed what you might have preferred to take for granted.

In my opinion, two things motivate us: convenience and fear. And I'm as entitled to my opinion as the next guy, although I doubt the next guy (in this case inmate No. 86296) thinks about such things. I suppose I should never sell the next guy short, either. There's no telling what flash of genius will come to a person doing our kind of time.

For what we call progress—consider radial tires, for example, which don't go flat so much as they rely on a cataclysm to fail—there's always the temptation to look back with romantic detachment on simpler days. Nostalgia is the biggest charlatan there is.

The governor of our state, Busey "Bus" Odums, was so affected when he ran for office on a platform recommitting Georgia to that venerable and dusty tradition known as the chain gang. He would have brought back the electric chair, too, if the legislature had allowed it. During his most recent campaign he posed with an ax and was quoted in the *Journal Constitution* as saying he was ready to cut down the tree and to build and wire the device himself.

Bus was first elected governor in the mid-seventies as a Democrat, when the South was still barely the South, and again two years ago as a Republican, having sat on the sidelines for a generation and been witness to the undoing of the mythic world of his boyhood. The rest of the country had stolen everything freaky from the homeland and tried to make it fashionable; they imposed a standard of correct behavior on its shortcomings and continued to mock whatever was left over. Along the way, they changed the flags. When the idea to revive the chain gang occurred to Bus, he must have reckoned it better to sin by executive order than ask permission and risk being told no.

He was present on the first of June as they separated forty-eight of us into groups of six, shackled at the waist, in a clearing behind the Sumter County jail. The Honorable Mr. Odums wore a seersucker blazer and toquilla straw hat, which he must have thought suited the occasion. He was on the verge of becoming legendary. In the sixties, Bus had been a football hero at the University of Georgia. After a career in real estate and a stint in the legislature, he became the governor best remembered for paving twenty-five hundred miles of rural highway and putting up-to-date textbooks into the hands of Georgia's school children. Bus called it his "black-and-white initiative," which was something of a play on words. He went to considerable effort to make it known that primarily black districts would get the same new books as primarily white ones, not just the latter's hand-me-downs. A decade after his first stay in the executive mansion, Bus was the man credited with securing the 1996 Olympics for Atlanta and the only person in America, it seemed, who wasn't surprised when a redneck set off a bomb.

Standing in the shade between a pair of grizzled oaks (They had lined us prisoners up in the sun.), Bus Odums seemed to have gotten shorter over the years but had grown in girth to match his wife, Carrie, who had always been large. Carrie, also present, was a relentless campaigner, and Bus couldn't get too much of her support. "Women like Carrie," he used to boast privately, "and women vote. A big woman don't threaten nobody," he would say. "She makes the thin ones feel thinner and the big ones feel better about themselves."

In addition to those of us who had come from Dooly State Prison in Unadilla, they imported offenders from Lee, Crisp, and Schley Counties just to have enough men to make for a respectable photo-op or to get any kind of work done. In place of our customary orange jumpers, we had been dressed in black-and-white striped work suits for the occasion. The suits were bright and new and well starched, yet they seemed baggy even on the largest members of our detail. The inmates from the neighboring counties had not changed before arriving, which presented a problem only until a man named Lawton Coles stepped forward to open his hardware store so they could get dressed, two at a time, in the men's room, while a pair of armed deputies waited outside. For as long as I stood there, Mr. Coles would not stop yammering about how happy he was to be of service.

"I want to thank y'all for comin'," the governor said. He took several steps forward. Although he was only yards away, Bus was clearly talking to everyone but us. "Today, we reclaim a tradition as time-honored and sacred as justice herself. For just as these men have torn down society, so then, as part of their penance, shall they build up society." I had heard as recently as that morning the part of society we would be building up was a stretch of Highway 30 between Route 45 and Friendship, Georgia—north and west of the county seat, Americus. It was a reboot of the roads program first undertaken by the same Busey Odums thirty years earlier and a length of pavement that had not been repaired since.

The governor approached the first row of prisoners. He examined us without looking. "All hard work brings a profit, but mere talk leads only to poverty, and so I charge these men to work for their own gain, for their own betterment, and at the same time to serve as an example to others that the State of Georgia will not stuffer intransigence." The bystanders applauded while photographers moved in, positioning for a good shot.

Other than the journalists, there was a handful of politicians and some local folks present—an oddball caucus of men and women, a few of whom looked like they had been stitched together from humankind's mismatched parts.

When Governor Odums finished his speech, a tumbledown bus groaned up the hill from behind Coles' Hardware. "Crisp County Department of Corrections" was stenciled in black letters on its side. It was the largest of the vehicles there and the one designated to transport us to the worksite. The governor and his wife posed for pictures with some county dignitaries before taking questions from the media. One of the younger reporters, seizing on a different angle, positioned himself near the door of the bus where two deputies were stationed—one on each side. The officer on the left looked like a boy scout and the one on the right looked like he weighed as much as three men. Both clutched rifles.

"What's your name?" the reporter asked. He was talking to the young one, whose wan face was largely hidden by a pair of dollar-store aviators. An inch-wide gap hung open between his neck and the collar of a pressed blue shirt.

"Deputy Giles," the boy said. I could tell he was nervous, unsure if he should be talking to the media or doing anything other than counting prisoners. The first two rows of six had boarded to the steady percussion of chains on chains. My group was next.

"I need your first name," the reporter said. "For the paper."

"Dillon," he said. The other deputy glanced over.

120

"You done this kind of work long?"

"Naw sur," Dillon said. "The chain gang's new."

"There's nothin' new about it," the reporter said. "I mean how long have you done law enforcement."

"Long 'nough."

"What do think about all this?" he asked.

"Not my place to say," Deputy Giles answered.

"These are dangerous criminals, son," the reporter said. "Have you thought about what you'll do if one of these men tries to escape?"

"Naw sur," Dillon said with the confidence of one whose orders had been made clear. "No need to think. If somebody tries to escape, I'll shoot um."

II

I don't consider myself a dangerous criminal. A criminal, yes, having stood before a judge once for a sentencing just as Bus Odums had twice for a swearing in. I'm guilty, and I'll admit it, which is more than my colleagues in chains would do. But not dangerous. I had, however, given some thought to trying to escape, so I suppose it was to my advantage to have heard the reporter's question asked and answered. I wondered if the boy had it in him to shoot a man or if he had volunteered for the detail because he was looking for an opportunity to do so.

When the last row of prisoners was seated, eight deputies boarded—four in back and four in front, backward facing, their rifles cradled over their hearts. I had thought about trying to escape. I was still thinking about it, but how lucky can a man get in a day? It was an accident of fate that Bus Odums had not recognized me. There were only four other white men on the detail, four among those who had jumped at day-for-day credit, time outside, and a chance to make a break for it should the opportunity present itself. There was not a man among us who wasn't thinking the same thing, but not one who would have said as much. We may all have been criminals, but I doubt any of us was that stupid.

Nine miles outside of Americus the bus began to shimmy over buckles in the road. When the vehicle stopped, we were discharged alongside mile marker 70. Whether it was seventy miles to or from civilization's next outpost hardly seemed to matter, since under the blaze of an early summer sun our dystopia was complete.

"Farmland north. Peanuts. Beans," said the boy deputy, who on the ride seemed to have matured into someone in charge. "Wasteland east and west. Swampland south." Gripping his rifle by the stock, he used the barrel to point out distant and unseen topographies. "Gators," he added. "Snakes." With the reporters and the dignitaries and the onlookers gone, our circumstance felt newly grave. Now, with no one watching, instead of posing with these officers we were entrusted to them. The deputy's meaning was clear—there would be no escape since there was no place to escape to.

They separated each group of six by two hundred yards and into rows across the highway. From front to back the entire detail spanned less than a mile. The first of each two lines used sledgehammers to even out potholes, passing slabs of broken pavement hand over hand to the shoulder. The next row was fed a steady soup of molten asphalt via conveyors from the backs of dirty orange trucks: bitumen heated to 300°. I was on the fourth row back, third from the left, in the middle of the highway. Like the others in my line, I was given a rake for spreading asphalt. Plumes of heat rose in columns that seared my eyes—hotter than the sun on my neck or the ooze of pitch burning through my boots. The heady smell of oil and gas came in waves. Worst of all, there was no way to track time. At least two men fainted before they pulled us to the roadside for lunch. My work suit had doubled in weight, soaked top to tail in sweat.

There was no shade along the clay embankment, no relief of any kind on either side of Highway 30. No. 86296 ate his bologna sandwich in two bites. When he lay back against the earthwork, one of the deputies lumbered by and pressed a foot into his stomach. The bologna came back up intact.

"You couldn't treat no dog like this," said the man on my other side, looking at me as if I had been the one made to disgorge his lunch. Or perhaps, because I was white, he wondered if the deputy would have done the same to me. In prison, where nothing escapes notice, race escapes it least of all.

"Arcturus," he introduced himself, meeting me eye-to-eye. The two of us constituted the middle in our row of six. Equal yet opposite.

"Lawrence," I said, "and at least a dog would get some water with his bologna." As I pondered the meat, gravel-dusted on the ground, I imagined Bus Odums and whatever toothsome delights he might be enjoying, and where: United Daughters of the Confederacy's quarterly meeting at the Peachtree Hilton. Linen napkins ablaze with silver flatware, a menu of iced oysters in cucumber mignonette, rock shrimp salad, sweet tea, and air so intolerably cold it stiffened joints; or a State Republican Party fundraiser, perhaps, alfresco, at a downstate Rotary Club, where he would make a few indiscrete remarks to rile up a redneck base before sitting down to freshwater catfish, hushpuppies, coleslaw, and cold beer.

Arcturus brought me back to reality. "Is you all right?" He was careful not to ask like he cared too much, but when a man is chained to you there is the implication that your fate is also his

123

own. If I were about to die, I expect Arcturus would want to know. But I had only drifted off and was heartbroken to find myself in the same dusty hole, a deputy from Sumter County kicking the lead man in each line until we were all back on our feet. Back on our feet and back to work.

Plenty of daylight remained by the time they called us off again. That was the first curiosity. The second was that while forty-eight of us had gone out, only forty-five were on the bus when it headed back. We had not left the work zone before I understood why: two ambulances, newly arrived, one on either side of the highway.

The plan was to keep the entire detail together at the Sumter County jail. After orchestrated showers and a change of clothes, they locked us up by pairs in the same order in which we worked the chain gang. Arcturus and I spent an hour together in our cell before the boy-deputy arrived to take twenty of us to the cafeteria.

"Ya'll is B group," he said. "A group's already eaten."

"You think they's dead?" Arcturus asked me that night. I don't know how he knew I wasn't asleep; it was like we were still bound together, bunk-to-bunk, by a chain of consciousness. The cornbread we'd been given at supper sat like a brick in my stomach and I lay awake, studying the moon as it passed between the bars of our cell's only window.

"We'll know if they don't send us out tomorrow," I said.

"Huh?"

"The chain gang's supposed to be hard time, not a death sentence."

"So, you don't think they's dead?"

"If they chain us together in the morning," I said, "you'll know nobody's dead."

"What's you in fo'?" Arcturus asked.

I had learned to expect this question and knew, when another prisoner asks, it means one of two things: If he's bigger than you, he's sizing you up. If he's smaller, he's hoping you'll ask him the same to give him a chance to brag. Given that, there are three reasons I never tell the truth. First, it's nobody's business. Second, I never feel like explaining what securities fraud is, and third, even with an explanation, it sounds weak—white-collar and assailable. While I doubted anyone would believe they'd put a man convicted of murder on an outdoor work detail, I was willing to take the chance. "I killed a man," I said.

"Damn." Arcturus kicked the bottom of my bunk. "Remind me not to fuck with you. Drugs," he said, without being asked. It's what I would have guessed. It was almost always drugs.

"So, you don't think they's dead?"

"I said I don't know."

It would have been a damn good maneuver if someone were trying to escape, I thought, falling asleep. Easy enough to feign exhaustion and get unchained before being carted off to a country hospital that wasn't prepared for prisoners. I cursed myself for not having thought of it ahead of time. The poor bastards probably had heatstroke after all, and here I was, fitter than most, losing my edge. The deputies would not have seen it coming, but I was sure they would make whatever adjustments were needed before taking us out again.

Sure enough, the next morning's detail started early to avoid the worst of the day's heat. We were given biscuits and coffee before dawn and all forty-five of us were back on-site by six a.m. Two ambulances, like sentinels, were there when we arrived.

Progress on the road was slow but not imperceptible. There was a sign several miles ahead, which, when I closed one eye, came somewhat into focus. With forward motion it became more distinct—square with white letters on a green field. Other than mile markers, it was the only sign we had seen on Highway 30, and it became my goal to get close enough to read it before the day's work was finished.

They fed us early. It must have been around ten. Not long after we got back to work, the sky grayed and let loose a steady shower. It was not one of those squalls that blasts its way through, but a cool, even rain. Steam meandered above the new asphalt, and dust rose from endless tracts of land on both sides of the highway. The work continued, and to look at Arcturus's face I could not have distinguished rain from sweat from tears. The humidity would be a curse if the sun came out, I thought, and by noon that's exactly what happened.

They called us off a second time, now to banks of mud. Some of the men grumbled that they wanted more bologna sandwiches, but the congress of deputies had huddled to discuss, I imagined, other things.

The sun beat down. They gave us water, but by the time we got back to the road the heft of air made it feel like we were supporting all heaven on our backs. The six of us in my line should have made a run for it when the deputies' backs were turned. What would they have done? Shoot us? Of course they would have. All six. Me, Arcturus, No. 86296, and the others. And so what? We'd be dead now, as dead to the past as to this foolish experiment as to the fantasy things were going to get better.

Several hours later, when one of the ambulances crept along the shoulder to a line ahead of us, I wondered who had collapsed and if that had become the acknowledged standard for a full day's work. Several minutes later, as slowly as it had come, the ambulance was in retreat. One of the deputies followed behind, hoisting his rifle to call us in. As we shuffled off the road, I looked up. To my left was the sign, near enough I almost could have touched it. How we had gotten so close so fast was a mystery of lost time. But there it was. A sign—a prophecy that would have done Ozymandias proud: GEORGIA'S HIGH TECH CORRIDOR. With fields beyond and a vault of sky above, I wondered if progress here was forthcoming or if we had missed it or if this was a reverse mirage, where instead of seeing things that weren't there we were missing things that are. My head swooned to bridge a physical nothing with a philosophical nothing. *What has been will be again. What has been done will be done again. There is nothing new under the sun.*

III

When the last man from B group was seated for supper, Deputy Giles pulled out a chair and stood on it. He was poised to make a production of news we had already gotten from A group: the chain gang was finished. When attorneys from the Southern Poverty Law Center had gotten wind of what was happening in Sumter County, the legal motions began flying. Less than twenty-four hours after the first newspaper account was published, a federal judge in Atlanta issued an injunction, and when the press learned a handful of inmates had been hospitalized, there came rumblings of civil litigation aimed at officials up to and including the governor. None of that was explained to us, of course, but information gets spread around a jail faster than cigarettes.

Those bound for Dooly State Prison, including Arcturus and me, would leave the next day, and earlier than the rest. We would be back in the yard before lunch, while the county inmates would be made to wait for their respective busses and so would "get there when they get there." This much we were told, before Deputy Giles got down off the chair.

"If we'd been organized," Arcturus said that night, "we could've ran for it."

"When?"

"Today. When them officers' backs was turned."

"You think so?" I said.

"I do."

"What about the other four?"

"That's why I say if we'd been organized."

"We'd be dead," I said, "instead of going back to prison."

I had never seen Arcturus at the penitentiary and probably wouldn't once we returned. He must have known it, and it was either this or the early end to Bus Odums' dalliance that had him ginned up and speaking freely.

"What about our day-for-day credit?" he asked. Arcturus wasn't the brightest man I had met in prison, but he wasn't the dullest by far.

"What about it?" I said. Through the window, the sky was wide with stars.

"Tell me somethin'," Arcturus said.

"What?"

"You ain't kill nobody."

"How do you know?"

"I know," he said.

Overnight, a short bus arrived from Dooly State Prison. It was still predawn when we were up and dressed. Someone from the Sumter County jail had decided those bound for the penitentiary did not need breakfast. The faster they could get rid of us, it seemed, the better.

"I'ma call my lawya," Arcturus murmured while we were being ushered out single file into the fusty blue air. "No breakfast."

We were still made to wear the black-and-white striped uniforms, but were now shackled in front by leg irons and handcuffs with no chains between us. We weren't on the road long before the sun came up. It was like we were bound for it, traveling due east on Highway 27. We'd been seated in cellblock order, which put Arcturus and me together, directly behind the driver.

The only two guards on the bus grazed on donuts from a box they passed between them, but offering none to the driver, who protested this as well as the fact he had not gotten enough sleep the night before.

"I can eat 'n' drive," he said. He was a thin old man, frail, with white hair and a constellation of liver spots running up both arms. Neither of the guards had been part of the original detail. From what I gleaned of their conversation, they had been sent to relieve two others, but their job now was to be as simple as fetching us from Americus and bringing us back to Unadilla.

"I can eat 'n' drive," the old man swore again. The bus rocketed down the highway, violating the centerline.

"Reg-you-lations," objected the lead officer, his mouth full. He was standing ahead of the standee line. His partner, seated across the aisle from us, laughed.

When there were no more donuts, there came a debate about whether at Drayton they should stay on 27 to Vienna and then take 41 through Pinehurst or head north to 329 via Byromville. All three agreed to avoid Interstate 75.

"Unless we wanna be back in twenty minutes," the driver said, "so 'en they can find more work for us."

"A-men," said the guard who stood, jockeying around the front of the bus.

"That's right," said the other. "Take 41."

Prior to sentencing, I was made to sit in court, where impact statements were read by my victims. Those I had swindled. After the first few, they began to sound the same. After a dozen, the judge called it quits because, I think, he realized they were. I wasn't sure if this was done to punish me or to allow the victims some relief. Probably it was a bit of both.

They had trusted me then, which made it easy—*yes* to the prospect of double-digit returns—*yes* to my outperforming sectors, markets, and money managers with whom they had worked for years.

No one of repute showed up for my sentencing. There were news trucks, cameras, and reporters, but Busey Odums, the once and future governor, most notable among my victims, didn't show. Rather, the tight shots were of some women's gnarled hands, which shook as they clutched notes. And they were women, mostly. The husbands of those not widowed stood diffidently behind, as wrecked as their legacies. It was the women who were the strong ones, steeled to confront me with the hardship I had brought upon them. People who had once been on the verge of a comfortable retirement were now coping with the shame of having to move in with their children. "I'm too old to work," one woman said. "I don't have time. I'm too old." "I'm on food stamps now," another said, until, overcome with emotion, she could not go on.

I felt bad for them, but managed well enough by reminding myself their own greed had made it possible. Not one didn't think I was cheating—they just didn't think I was cheating them. This was enough of a consolation until an 8'x10' cell at 'Villa

Unadilla' replaced my 6,500 square foot condo in downtown Atlanta.

We read newspapers in prison (Nobody's ever hanged himself with a newspaper.) and magazines, once the staples are removed. After sentencing, my name faded from headlines. Three years later I was so forgotten that I hardly recognized myself, until one afternoon I came across an article about a man in his sixties, Mr. Jay Stoops, who had shot his wife before killing himself. My name was mentioned briefly. The couple had been nearly wiped out. Mrs. Stoops had gotten sick and, having finally lost everything, they became homeless. According to the article, the gun he used was stolen.

The bus jerked violently, like an amusement ride, bouncing us in our seats. "Tell me somethin'," Arcturus said.

"What?" I said.

"You ain't kill nobody."

"Didn't I?"

North of Pinehurst the driver became downright cross. The lead man, still standing, had refused to allow a stop for a bathroom break. "Reg-you-lations," he kept saying.

"It ain't regulations to stand up at the front of the bus!" The old man gunned the engine. "It ain't regulations to take any ol' road y'all want back t' Unadilla!"

"Easy there, feller," the second officer said. "You'll enervate yerself."

Suddenly there was a low bang and the vehicle shimmied right. The driver lurched forward to steady the wheel. He hit the brakes. The front right tire pitched off the road, hurling the lead officer into the door. The second guard braced himself, groping for his gun.

The bus came to rest upright but at a hard lean off the highway. Several prisoners had been deposited in the aisle.

"You all right?" The second guard was addressing the lead man, sprawled in the door well. But it was the driver who answered.

"I—I think so," he said, draped over the column. "We blew a tire!"

"Jim, you all right?" the second guard said, drawing his weapon.

"Get 'em out the back," Jim hollered from below. "Face down . . . in a line!"

The driver was fidgeting with the radio. At first, on both sides of the highway, all I saw were trees—pitch pine and long leaf. A tractor-trailer blew by, laying on its horn.

The second guard held up his gun, above his head where it could be seen, and ordered every prisoner into a seat. He maneuvered to the rear, opened the emergency door, and jumped out. The bus began to empty of men broad-striped and shackled at the ankles, their hands bound together in front in the manner of those who pray. From where Arcturus and I sat, they looked like paratroopers, crouching then disappearing one after the other from the back of a plane. I was by the window, directly behind the driver, and through the thicket I suddenly spotted a lush, open field of green, the likes of which I had not seen in years. There, the earth seemed stitched in rows of emeralds.

"You go first," Arcturus said. There was a dreadful look on his face, as real as if he were indeed readying to jump from a great height.

I angled past.

The lead man, Jim, had not moved. "I think it's broke," he said to the driver.

Whatever "it" was didn't much matter to me, until I was halfway down the aisle. When I turned back, Arcturus had reached over the seat and wrapped the chain between his cuffs around the driver's neck.

"Now drive!" I heard Arcturus say. I shuffled the rest of the way to the back of the bus, pulled closed the door, and locked it. "Drive!" he said again.

"I can't," the old man gasped. The cuffs' ratchets pulled the flesh from his neck up and beneath both ears. Except for the fact he was being choked to death, the driver might have said what I was thinking: the tire was blown and the bus was going nowhere.

"Don't you do it," I warned the lead officer grimacing to draw his weapon. Ahead of us, in the distance, came the wail of sirens. But there was still time—time to take the guns and the keys and make a run for it, through the trees to the Promised Land or in the opposite direction, where the woods went on and on.

But with each moment, our prospects dimmed. The second officer, who had been preoccupied with the other prisoners, realized what was happening and began pounding on the back door. Read my mind, Arcturus, I thought, frozen in place. It's just us now. Read my mind while there's still a way.

"Give me your gun," I shouted at the lead officer, "or he'll kill him!"

"OK," he said, slowly raising his weapon.

"Drive!" Arcturus ordered, and he began to tighten his grip on the old man. How could he fail to understand our situation? How could anyone be so close to having his life back only to return to prison?

"Easy now," the officer said, the gun firmly in hand, the barrel oscillating between Arcturus and me.

"Drive!" Arcturus yelled. And that was when I realized he was a step ahead—brighter than I'd given him credit for. He had found his own path and taken it, a path to a history that does not repeat.

A plane of blue lights broke the horizon and Arcturus loosened his grip only to pull back with ferocious strength. The old man's face was the color of a plum.

"Drive!" he screamed, turning the back of his head to the officer, giving him the clear shot and no choice but to take it. "Drive! Drive! Drive!"

That Old-Time Religion

And these signs shall attend them that believe; In my name shall they cast out devils; they shall speak with new tongues; They shall take up serpents; and if they ever drink any deadly thing; it shall not hurt them; they shall lay hands on the sick, and they shall recover.
~ Mark 16:17–18

IN THE EARLY DAYS of his father's church and as a show of faith and humility before God, the congregation handled snakes, a practice that, at the time, was no more unusual to Ethan Krugley's father's flock than using dogs to hunt or mules to plow a field. On most Thursday nights, those lowest of animals served the highest of purposes at the New Life Church of Christ in Bear Stand, Tennessee. It was all quite regular business, though whatever handling was to be done was taken care of by Idem Potts, the deacon, or Colonel Stall.

From spring through autumn, the men spent Monday afternoons scaring up a specimen or two, usually a cottonmouth or rattlesnake, from one corner or another of Unincorporated Carter County—in the highlands or by the river, where there was standing water and debris. Then, three nights later, the congregation would form two lines and slog in pairs up to the sanctuary to gently run their fingers over several inches of the snakes' slick, scaly skin.

The local coloreds thought this was crazy. As much stomping and clapping and carrying on for the Lord as took place at the First African Church, there probably wasn't a snake for miles.

As it turned out, Ethan never touched a snake, nor was there the expectation he would, even if his father was the pastor or perhaps for that reason. Some, it seemed, were beyond proving needful of God's protection, and if children and prophets are to be counted separately, Ethan might have been doubly exempt. For his part, the boy was always more suspicious of those who fooled with the snakes than those who did not. If this was anything like a backwoods confessional, he thought, the folks who presented themselves must be the ones most in need of forgiveness or those with the most to hide.

Potts and Stall called it "dancing," the way they swayed from side to side on the balls of their feet, holding each serpent behind its head at arm's length from their bellies.

"Praise God's mighty hand," they hummed in an even key.

"Praise Jesus," sighed the ladies, who came up more often than the men to stroke the snakes.

In more than fifty years of worship, not a righteous soul got bit.

By the time Ethan answered the call to preach, he had already had half a dozen jobs and spent a decade living in Knoxville, where he was briefly enrolled at the East Tennessee Bible College. He first came home when Idem Potts passed away. Even though Idem was the youngest of his father's friends, he was the first to enter glory. It had been a heart attack, they said, or a stroke, or a touch of both. His wife was visiting her sister in Wilber when it happened, and by the time one of the farm hands found him on the kitchen floor, Idem had been dead a week.

Eight years later, when Colonel Stall went looking for one of his dogs after dusk and fell three hundred feet into a crevasse, Ethan had tired of the city and decided it was time to move home once and for all. Even though the Colonel was old, his death, because it had been an accident, came as a shock. Ethan figured it also meant that once his father passed, he would have to decide what to do about the church.

All the while, the ritual with the snakes continued. Jackson Potts took over after his father died, and Reverend Krugley replaced the Colonel with a hayseed named Danny Atterberry, twenty years younger than Ethan, who couldn't get enough of trapping and handling, especially after *The Walnut Ridge Examiner* visited to Bear Stand to do a feature on the practice. Although the boy was as poor as dirt, he walked around for months like a celebrity.

Once he arrived at Ethan's house unannounced. He was a gawky kid, slick and taut, and had been told Ethan's disinterest in handling snakes extended to capturing them. "Wanna go with me up to the bluff?"

"What bluff?" Ethan said, more from boredom than desire. It was late February. Following four days of snow, the world around them was wholly frozen. To complicate matters, Ethan and his father had been arguing. Reverend Krugley had asked his son to preach for the first time that Sunday, and Ethan told him he'd rather dance with snakes than give a sermon.

"Rough Ridge," Danny said, turning off the engine but not bothering to get out of his daddy's truck. He was wearing a blue and white mesh cap and looked no older than his age—fourteen.

"Isn't that where the Colonel fell off?"

"I dunno," Danny said. He was always surprisingly clean, Ethan noticed, for someone who wasn't in school and didn't have money. His face was soft and pale, with a jaw resembling a sickle and hair like crests of new wheat tapered over dark, almond-shaped eyes.

"What do you wanna go up there for?" The boy didn't answer. He just slouched behind the wheel of the Chevy. "I guess," Ethan consented. "Just to clear my head. Take Laurel Fork?"

"Far's we can," Danny said. "Then up Ridge Gap."

"That way clear?" Ethan asked, climbing into the cab. To him it felt colder inside the truck than out.

"I reckon not," Danny said. "But if not, we'll clear it."

The narrow step up Ridge Gap had not been cleared, so Danny plowed through two feet of snow. The truck hugged the embankment, and all four tires spun deep. He parked near the top of the mountain, in a clearing surrounded by woods on three sides and rock face on the fourth. Bare, black trees grew close together, splintering into a tarnished sky. From where they stood, a pure, white skirt rolled out in all directions.

"We'll walk from here," Danny said. He cut the engine and got out. The landscape was perfect, silent and still. The boy sauntered around back and slid a .22 from beneath a tarp in the bed of the truck.

"Where to?"

"Don't matter, does it? It's all God's country."

"Why do you need a rifle in God's country?" Ethan asked.

For twenty minutes they forged a pass one-half mile north and east over dead and fallen trees and through shin-deep drifts. It was slow going, like walking underwater.

"Even the Devil finds himself a place in God's country," Danny lifted the rifle to his shoulder, sighting something distant or imaginary.

They walked another hundred yards, up a steep grade, pulling themselves forward by branches that jutted from the snow. As one snapped free in Ethan's hand, he fell back onto the path.

"C'mon," the boy said, turning and offering a hand. He said it like he knew where they were going, and indeed Ethan hoped he did. Except for their tracks, which were already being blown over, he had little idea how to get back to the truck.

"There," Danny said, pausing and angling his face to the sky. With the gun's barrel, he gestured east and led the way cautiously. "So what are ya gonna talk about?"

"Pardon?"

"On Sunday. Ain't your pa ask you to preach?"

"Maybe." It was irksome to Ethan that Danny knew his business.

"Preach about!" The boy stopped cold. "Preach about! That's what I meant to say." He grinned, like he was embarrassed, then took off the mesh cap and tousled his hair. "Lots of folks talk. Talkin's what we're doin' now. But preachin'—preachin's altogether different."

Not far ahead, in the direction they were moving, the horizon brightened where it seemed to be freakishly out of alignment with the surrounding landscape.

"Hadn't thought about it," Ethan said.

The boy waited for him to pass. "Best not think," Danny said, leaning the rifle against a tree then removing his shirt and jacket over his head in a single motion. "Let the Holy Ghost speak through you," he said, hoisting the gun. "That's one thing's different 'tween talkin' and preachin'."

A shot split the sky—a crack far louder than the sound of the branch that had snapped off in Ethan's hand. The boom hung in the air for several seconds, echoing off of snow and rock.

"What the—!" Ethan watched Danny, the gun still level with his bare shoulder and a thin trail of smoke coiling around the muzzle. "What are you shooting at?"

"Nothin' in partic'lar."

"Where's your shirt? Are you crazy? You'll freeze." Ethan couldn't take his eyes off of the boy, and he imagined the peculiar nature of the circumstance gave him license to stare.

"C'mon," Danny said. "Look-a here." He ambled ahead to a line in the snow where the earth split for dozens of yards in front of them. The gorge was tremendous, the plunge spectacular. It was a sheer drop, hundreds of feet to boulders that appeared no larger than nickels.

"Wow," Ethan said. He was no longer watching the boy but rather this formidable drop, testing the ground as he clutched a pine at the cliff's edge. Everything—rocks, trees, and the gully below were frosted white. "If you didn't know this was here, you'd hardly see it coming."

"That's why I like it," Danny said. He moved as close to the edge as one could get, until his bare arm brushed Ethan's jacket. "To test the flesh."

"Is that why you're half undressed?"

"Well," the boy grinned, "why do you think we came here?" It was a question to which, it occurred to Ethan, there might be several answers. "I wanna be a deacon in God's church," Danny proclaimed. "One day. When you take over." Ethan checked the impulse to ask if he was serious, although some doubt must have shown on his face. "I know Jackson's older and that his pa was deacon, but Jackson don't want it and I do! The Lord's strong in me, Ethan. You'll see!" As Danny spoke, with the toe of his left foot he dug up a stone from the snow at the base of the pine and sent it over the cliff. It seemed to fall in slow motion, like it could fall forever.

"I thought you brought me here to trap snakes."

"*Snakes?*" Danny cocked his head, his brown eyes wide. "In winter? You gotta be kiddin'. The nearest you'll find to a snake up here in February's me or you."

Reverend Krugley died on November 17th, his birthday. Two years had passed, during which Ethan began to inherit the church as if it was a kind of birthright or family curse. It began with what mattered most, the preaching. Near the end, and when it appeared his father might exit the world on the same date he had entered it, the pastor pleaded with his son to shoot him, or keep him alive for a few more hours, or engrave a lie on his headstone. As reason failed, Reverend Krugley worried aloud that having the same dates above his grave would make him seem trivial to posterity. This was the cause of some distress, until Ethan convinced his father such a coincidence might be interpreted differently.

"I can't think of a better birthday present, can you, than to claim a place in our Father's house? That's what folks'll say." If nothing else, the idea gave his father something new to think about.

The next day, Reverend Krugley called Ethan to his bedroom. "I've been thinking about what you said, and as best I can see you've got a point—that piece about our Father's house." His expression was wizened. It was etched with pain. "The Lord hath sent me a son to carry on His work." Ethan sat at the foot of the bed. "But Ethan . . . them snakes," he said, rolling his eyes. "If they mock us with anything, it'll be them damn snakes. Promise me, when I'm gone, you'll get done with that."

"I promise," he said.

After his father had taken to bed, Ethan only continued with the service out of deference. But times were changing, and the church too must change.

"Is it cold in here to you?" his father asked.

"Should I throw more wood on?"

"Yes."

Ethan went outside to fetch some of the birch Danny had split that morning. It took less than five minutes, but by the time he got the logs into the stove and returned to the bedroom, his father was gone.

After worship on Thanksgiving, the men of the church council met and in twenty minutes formally elected Ethan to take his father's place. It would have gone quicker except that Jupiter Ramsey came late.

Three years earlier, Reverend Krugley shocked the congregation by insisting there be a black man, chosen from the community, to serve on council. Recently, this had been Jupiter. As usual, nobody told him there was going to be a meeting, and when he happened to show up it was to get a share of the turkey dinner the charity guild prepared annually for the needy. Cap Davenport was ready to force the issue and have the vote anyway, and he would have succeeded until Jupiter arrived and the point became moot.

Ethan knew why his father had instituted the policy of having a colored man on council. The elder Krugley had thought of himself as a visionary. He had a sense of where the world outside of Bear Stand was moving. Ethan figured this must also have been why his father felt the snake handling was so ridiculous. For different reasons, Ethan concluded they were both silly practices—having a black man on council because he wasn't wanted and fooling with snakes because, worse than being primeval, it was downright dangerous. The younger Krugley thought of himself not as a visionary but as a man of sense and reason. And there was no sense in any of this.

When he got home, Ethan found Danny waiting outside. He had a good idea what the boy wanted to discuss. "The Lord led

His people out of the wilderness," Ethan said, feeling like he was still in the pulpit. "Why are you so hot to drag us back into it?"

Danny looked at the ground. He had been chopping birch. His shirttail was out and his arms and neck were splayed with chips. "The snakes is a test."

"They're no test," Ethan scoffed. "No test that matters." The smell of roasted duck was in the air. "How old are you?"

"You know how old I am."

"How old?"

"Almost sixteen."

"When you turn sixteen, we can talk about making you a deacon."

This had in no way been Ethan's plan, and he thought about it no longer than it took him to say it.

"Really?"

"What's that smell?" Ethan said. "Did you make dinner?"

"Cleaned up, too."

"I thought you were just chopping wood. How'd you get in?"

"Broke in," Danny said. "You serious, I mean, 'bout makin' me deacon?"

"You broke in?"

"The Lord's strong in me."

"Did he teach you how to break into a house?"

"No, but it ain't hard. I turn sixteen in March, Reverend."

"Ethan," he snapped.

"Don't ya think if I'm gunna be deacon, I should call ya—"

"Ethan. And how did you break in?" Even as he asked, Ethan realized he didn't want to know. "Never mind. Let's say grace and eat."

He couldn't possibly ordain the boy. The idea was more ludicrous than handling snakes or having a black man on council.

Jupiter himself wouldn't approve such a decision, Ethan knew, taking the boy's hand to bless the food. Even in absentia.

Spring arrived and Ethan felt a kind of rebirth. He had grown into his new role, until preaching became like second nature. Over the winter, Reverend Krugley put down roots with the congregation, and his decision no longer to have a colored man on council went a long way toward winning over the older members of the parish.

Ethan had read in *Baptist Times* about something called a sabbatical, which sounded like a cross between a pilgrimage and a working vacation. Since the church would never have enough money to send him to the Holy Land, Reverend Krugley decided on Nashville. Faye Davenport wanted to know if Nashville was in a dry county. There were other questions, none of which rose to the level of objection. He would go for six weeks and be back in time for Easter, avoiding by design Danny's sixteenth birthday while also giving the boy time to come to terms with the fact that even though the snakes were coming out of hibernation, their services at the New Life Church of Christ would no longer be required.

Danny had already started showing up with trapping bags and plastic tubs in the back of his father's truck, and with the same .22, Ethan presumed, under the same tarp. He guessed the boy had started hunting about the time he stopped asking Ethan if he wanted to join him in the highlands.

"But they scare away mice," Danny added to a growing list of arguments made right up to the morning he drove Ethan to the bus station. "You ever see a mouse in that church?"

"When I'm gone, buy a cat."

"That'll be my first job as deacon?"

"What time's the bus?"

144

"I dunno. Ain't my bus. Can I come with you?"

Ethan had anticipated this.

"A boy like you? What would your father say, me taking you into that wilderness?"

"He's drunk. He don't care." The boy came alive, given the impression Ethan would consider it. "Besides, Nashville ain't no wilderness. This here's the wilderness."

"No, sir. You said it yourself. This is God's country. You been to the city?"

"Knoxville. Once."

"Knoxville doesn't count," Ethan said. "Knoxville's small potatoes."

"Take me with you. I done told you a hundred times. The Lord's strong in me. Take me with you an' you'll see!"

Ethan checked his watch as Danny veered down a side road where the Greyhound station came into view. The boy drove more slowly.

"Why are you slowing down? Can't you see they're loading the bus?"

"You don't never tell me the truth," Danny said. "Drive me here. Drive me there. Cook me this . . . chop my wood. But you don't take me serious."

"Listen—"

"No, you listen," said the boy, his mouth as straight as a razor. "You take away what matters and don't give me nothin' I care about."

"Like being a deacon in God's church."

"I'll be sixteen 'fore you get back—or did you forget?"

While Danny parked the truck and went to fetch the bags, Ethan hurried to have a word with the bus driver.

"Come with me," he ordered, motioning for the boy to leave the luggage and follow him into the depot.

Behind the counter, a bald man with sleepy eyes was reading a newspaper. Nearby, a fat woman scolded three small children. Everyone else, it seemed, had boarded.

"Bathroom?" Ethan asked the man behind the desk.

"Outside. Around back."

"C'mon." Reverend Krugley took Danny by the arm and led him around the cinderblock façade to a bathroom so foul it could have been a portal to the underworld. The door, off its hinges, had been set against one wall. Inside, the porcelain sink was stained with streaks of brown mold. All around was the smell of bowels purged.

"What're ya doin? You'll miss yer bus."

Reverend Krugley turned on the faucet, which hacked up air before a jet of cold, red water gushed forth.

"Danny Atterberry," he said, cupping the water in his hands, "I ordain you to a new life in Christ, and I call you to be a deacon in God's church."

Ethan spilled the water over the boy's thick, blonde hair. His fingers slid across the boy's ears and cheeks, his thumbs coming to rest at the edges of Danny's mouth.

"You honest?"

"But you have to say you want it."

"Pardon?"

"You've been called. Now you have to answer the call. Do you want it?"

"I do."

"All right then." He took his hands from the boy's face, which still seemed disbelieving, like he expected to feel different but did not. "When I get back, we'll do it right. In the sanctuary."

"What do I do 'til then?"

"I'll tell you what you *don't* do," Ethan said, getting to his point. "You don't tell anybody about this until I get home and the council hears it from me."

"That it?"

"No. There's something else," Ethan said, drying his hands on his pants and moving away from the makeshift font. "Don't you bring a single snake into my church when I'm gone. Do you hear me? Not one."

Much happened in forty days. There was a tornado, for one thing, in Coopers Township, north of Bear Stand. Trees were down for miles and in Unincorporated Carter County, too. The bus driver, who made the same trip three times a week, drove slowly enough that everyone could see the damage. Ethan, as he surveyed it from the Greyhound, was relieved to learn that no one, neither saint nor sinner, had been killed. The twister cleared a swath of forest along the south side of Rocky Knob, where thirty-foot pines were shorn in two like pencils. But none of this compared, Ethan thought, to the ruin he had witnessed in the city. The trees especially reminded him of this: souls shorn in two. He liked the image so well he wrote it down to use in Sunday's sermon.

Though he had not been sure what he was looking for in Nashville, Ethan's mission had found him. Like Christ in the wilderness, he came face-to-face with the sorest woe a mortal life can offer. From pride, to anger, to gluttony, he had stared them down and witnessed their temptations firsthand. He was entering his own Jerusalem now, in time for Easter, to testify to his own deliverance. Like Christ in Jerusalem, Ethan returned to Bear Stand in lowliness and humility. Jupiter Ramsey picked him up at the bus station, and he was back a full day before anyone else saw him.

On Saturday night, Reverend Krugley walked to the church, sat in the sanctuary, and prayed. Soon, the sacristy door opened. It was Anna May Moran, who had come with her mother, Ruth, to replace the red frontals of the passion with Easter white.

"Reverend," she said happily, "I didn't know you was back."

"Yesterday."

Mrs. Moran followed her daughter out. "Reverend Krugley!"

Ethan stood and embraced the elder Moran. "Blessings, Ruth. I understand you all had some excitement while I was away," he said with the storms in mind.

"You mean 'bout them snakes?" She rolled her eyes as if she might even be joking. "It was nothin' a child of God can't handle."

"Snakes?"

"Yes—oh, a week ago? Was that last week, Anna May," she asked, "or two weeks back? Anyhow, when they got loose o'ernight it was an unholy mess. Took Jackson Potts an' that boy you made deacon the better part of a day to gather 'em all back up."

"All?"

"Eight or so, I fig're. But ain't no harm done. They was back in their crates by the time the guest preacher come."

"Guest preacher?"

"The one Deacon Atterberry invited from Second Baptist in Braemar."

Ethan sat down, his face as red as the frontals still draped over the pulpit. "Any idea where Deacon Atterberry is now?"

"No. But don't be angry, Reverend," Ruth said. "That boy's some prophet! The Lord is strong in him. And who'd think it? All that passion stitched-up in such a little stalk of a thing,"

"Out of the mouth of babes," Anna May said, seeming almost smitten.

"He preached?"

"He called it witnessin'," Mrs. Moran raised her palms, as if needing to shield herself from the impression the boy had made. "But I call it preachin'." Ethan's skin blistered. "Don't be angry," she went on, "if it's 'bout the snakes. The guest preacher thought it was—" Ruth's face surveyed rows of the empty pews for the word he had used.

"Charismatic," Anna May supplied.

"That's right," Ruth picked up. "Said it was like that old-time religion. An' besides, like I said, there weren't no harm done."

It rained overnight and steadily into Easter morning. But weather doesn't slow the faithful, so by nine o'clock the church on Rural Route 41 was a full house. It was dark enough outside that the service seemed more vigil than festival.

Cap and Faye Davenport were there, and Ellie Bradford, and Erma and Jackson Potts, and Zack Humphreys, and the other farmers and their wives and children from the west side of the county. A few of the local colored folks showed up and sat in folding chairs or stood in back. But down in front, sitting between Ruth and Anna May Moran, was Danny—sixteen now and, as if to prove it, with the thinnest growth of down on his chin.

"The strife is o'er, the battle done," the pastor proclaimed, to quote from the hymn and begin his sermon. In the distance, thunder rolled. "I have been to the wilderness and back, my friends, and I have seen firsthand the needs of the world our risen Christ was sent to save." Ethan looked at the boy, whose eyes were already bargaining for forgiveness. "It's a world that tunes God out, sees only what it wants to see and hears only what it wants to hear. It's a world that buys more but has less, a world that consumes more but is less satisfied, a world of more convenience but less patience. I have confronted the tempter, answered the Devil, and said, 'Get thee behind me, Satan!'" A few muted "Amens" rose from the back of the building. "But the enemy is never where we expect him, yet ever before us, and here, in God's country, his wile is at its best because to win the souls of His most righteous is a mighty prize. But I tell you again, brothers and sisters in Christ, that today the strife is o'er, the battle done!"

"Amen!" came the shout again, with black and white alike raising their voices. That would show him, thought Ethan of the boy, who seemed as caught up in the sermon as the rest—how to preach the Word without props.

"That was some witness you gave," Danny said the next day. He had driven to Reverend Krugley's home to confront the inevitable. Ethan had been clearing the yard of debris, but stopped when he saw the familiar truck climbing the hill. "Was it that bad in the city?"

"Was what that bad?"

"The sin."

"No," he said, toweling his face. "Sin's about the same everywhere. The real difference is that out here there's more places for it to hide."

"You angry?" Danny asked.

"You mean about the snakes?"

"And 'cause I done told people you made me deacon in the sink."

Ethan surveyed the mountains, newly green. "Not so much," he said.

"Really?"

"I don't have anything against snakes. Not like you think."

"Really?"

"Except I don't think Reverend Krugley liked them." It felt odd for Ethan to speak of his father in this way, as one already so distant he presumed to know him better by reputation.

"Oh, I dunno," Danny said. "He liked 'em well enough." The boy went to the back of the truck, lowered the tailgate, and threw back the tarp to reveal four plastic tubs, hemp bags, a metal pole, and his gun. Inside one of the two opaque tubs, there appeared to be turf and loose sticks shifting of their own accord and producing a muted, ticking sound. "I was gonna let 'em loose. I thought you was gonna make me."

"I just don't know," Ethan said quietly.

"I was gonna drive you back to Rough Ridge and let you watch me do it. But if you want, we can go lookin' for more." The boy's jeans sagged to the balls of his hips as he leaned against the tailgate.

"All right," Ethan said. He looked around, then to the sky, and for the first time felt he and the boy were speaking the same language. "Let's go."

It had been two years and two months since their first venture into the woods. It was noteworthy to Ethan how little things had changed but how, in God's time, nothing ever does.

From the clearing, where tracts of mud had replaced tracts of snow, Reverend Krugley led the way up the side of the ridge using, he imagined, the same branches and roots as before. "You forget something?" he asked, glancing back.

"Such as?"

"Your gun?"

"I ain't forget it," Danny said. "Left it. Don't need a gun to trap snakes." Ethan pretended not to notice the boy was also without his other effects—the gunnysacks, pole, and tubs. "So, you ain't sore?" Danny said.

151

"What makes you think I am?" Ethan was nervous, and he was sure Danny thought forgiveness had come too easily. He stayed in front as they approached the point where they would leave the path.

"Even 'bout me preachin'?"

"This it?" Ethan asked.

"Deeper," said the boy, removing his shirt and tucking it like a flag into the back of his jeans. "That-a-way. If you're lookin' for the same spot."

Before he saw the break in the trees, Ethan heard the rush of meltwater, like static, echoing from the bottom of the canyon. In a few moments, the end was in view: a place where the world is broken and has been since the great flood.

"It's a sight," Danny said, hands on hips as he joined Ethan at the brink. But this time, Reverend Krugley was not so absorbed in the view as in the boy, whom he figured to be the real prophet, the real gift from God. "You see something you like?" Danny asked, to make clear the wild nature of the world—and his own nature—leaving no doubt about who he was, who Ethan was, or the end to which they were called.

"I . . ." Ethan raised his hands, to test the space between them.

"Don't talk," Danny said, taking Ethan's hands in his.

"I can't—"

"I ain't asking you to be who you ain't. Didn't take your pa half as long."

"*What?*" Ethan faltered, and a bolt of mud dislodged into the abyss.

"I told you. The Lord's strong in me. I'll do whatever to answer the call."

To Ethan the boy appeared as an altogether different creature now, worldly-wise and powerful. A perfect beast, a golden cow, a crown of flesh.

"I can see you're not," Danny said, sounding more determined than disappointed. The boy removed his hands. "All things in time," he prophesied.

Ethan stood dazed in the knowledge of what was and what was to be. Danny disappeared down the path, his blonde hair flickering then vanishing in the brush.

Reverend Krugley had a particular set of problems but found relief in the distraction they brought. He wondered if Danny would wait for him. Ethan hoped he would and yet prayed he would not. And if not, he worried about how to get back to Bear Stand and how, once there, everything, and yet nothing, will have changed.

Part Three

Voyageurs

THE EARTH DREW HIM IN, and Silas sank by his own weight. Silt stole between the toes of his right foot, over his calf and knee, and partway up his thigh. But he didn't panic. He steadied his body, one hand on the gunwale of the canoe and the other turning circles in the thin, Canadian air. When he found his balance, he recovered into the boat.

The Devil lives in the lake. This is what the *mangeurs de lard* believed, those yet uninitiated fur traders who either with or without an Ojibwe guide managed to survive their virgin pass through the wilderness before being called *voyageurs*. For Silas, at least, this first step was inauspicious. His Lab took no notice, continuing to gallop around the shore. Silas worried about Dollar. He and Meagan had had some trouble passing the nine-month-old over the border at International Falls. But getting him to the base camp at Backs Bay would be an altogether different challenge. Meagan insisted they bring vet papers, proof of vaccinations, and everything short of a canine passport—and this turned out to be a good decision since the border agents were more scrutinizing of Dollar than of either of them.

"I told you we'd need them," she said, securing her blonde hair behind both ears. "The papers, I mean." Meagan was not the self-righteous type, and Silas knew what his girlfriend was doing. She was laying the foundation to punish him for mistakes to come: a missed turn, a badly chosen campsite, a botched dinner, a longer than expected portage. A trip through the bush—even in a charted provincial park like Quetico—was nothing to be fooled with, and if there was such a thing as bunny slopes for boundary lakes, Quetico was not it. There would be surprises, and already

Silas had taken chances, like choosing to traverse the wilderness from south to north, ending at the outfitter's camp rather than starting there, and deciding to make the seven-day voyage without a guide.

"It's a good map," he said on the drive up, rapping it on the Jeep's dashboard. The chart was folded-over five times to exactly fit the dimensions of a large Ziploc.

"It's not the map I'm concerned about," Meagan said.

A boy named Cody, who was a twenty-year-old naturalist guide sent by the outfitter, met them on the Canadian side before adding to their provisions and taking the couple, via pontoon, to Prairie Por, north of Sucker Lake. He wore a too-small pink tee that had been red once. Authentic vintage. It was early September, the end of another season, and Cody would be on his way back to the university in Montreal after a final trip to base camp, where he had spent the summer leading student groups on short excursions through small circuits of the northern park—nothing like the week-long trip that lay ahead for the two Americans he was dropping off, one of whom he just watched bury a third of his body in silt even before taking a seat in the canoe.

"I can still come with you," he offered. "Harbor the boat and rent a canoe from town."

"We're fine," said Silas. He looked like he was wearing a black cast on his right leg, which hung over the starboard side as he tried to rinse off the mud.

"But thanks," Meagan said.

The previous night, and to enjoy some privacy, Silas and Meagan had locked Dollar in the hotel bathroom before having sex. Not that they wouldn't also make love on the trail—which was one more reason not to want Cody along. Silas had purchased a novelty book, *How to Have Sex in the Woods*, from a tourist shop in International Falls. He thought it was funny, but Meagan, when he showed it to her, looked like she wanted to grab the dog and return to St. Louis. Silas could tell when Meagan wasn't satisfied, when she was bored, but he had only bought the book as a joke. Surely she didn't think him so insecure as to consult a field guide for something like that. The sex, like everything between them, would be different in the wilderness— as a resolution to heated fights they'd have or as an ongoing experiment hatched in the spirit of discovery. It would be archetypal; in the canoe, on rocks, on top of a dam, or beside their campsite, under the stars and as a thank offering to the universe after he proposed and after she said yes.

Day One, Sunday

So much depended on the folded map, that illusion of control Silas kept with him in the bow of the canoe. When he and Cody had been alone with the poster-sized chart unfurled, they studied routes. The boy's angular fingers traced paths across the smooth surface of the map, where images of lakes were connected by thin red lines, each a portage. Some were named and with a number alongside to indicate the length the meters: North Por 670, Singing Brook Por 470, Yum Yum Por 1230, *Portage des Morts* 460, Have a Smoke Por 300.

"If you get lost," he said. "What I mean is if something happens to the map, stay in open water and travel north as far as you can and then west until you can go north again. Do you have a compass?"

"No."

"Ha, really?" Cody said. "Then mark it out by the North Star. Eventually you'll hit either Pickerel or Batchewaung." He indicated the two largest lakes at the northernmost edge of the

159

park. "We can find you there if you're not in camp by Saturday afternoon."

"Should we expect choppers and a flotilla?" Silas asked.

"More like T-Joe and me in a canoe." Cody, who was taller and thinner than Silas, seemed incapable of offense. His careless grin shone bright against tan features, his tousled hair as thick as Meagan's and as black as hers was gold. T-Joe, Silas surmised, must be another of the outfitter's troop of model-ready naturalist guides. "Here now," Cody said. "Eat this."

"What is it?"

"Pork," the boy said, passing him a ribbon of meat as thick as the spine on a book. The plastic wrapper was already peeled back. "There's more in your pack. It's tradition to eat pork before you set out. You and the girlfriend."

"For luck?"

"No, but a compass might have helped with that," Cody said, placing the jerky in Silas's hand. "It's tradition. I can't be responsible for what might happen if you don't."

"What are you willing to be responsible for if we do?" Silas said. "Besides, we're vegetarian."

"Think of it as a ritual then," Cody said. "A ceremony."

Silas pulled the wrapper further down and took a large bite. "Between you and me," he said, "I never stopped loving meat. But you'll have no luck with her." He handed back the rest. "She's as faithful as they come."

Twenty minutes into Bayley Bay, Silas moved the map from the thwart of the canoe to a place between his feet. In St. Louis, he managed investment portfolios. He could predict the behavior of markets with good success, but for Silas, the most stalwart tables of the past, those constant and reliable cycles of heaven, were unsolvable mysteries. He knew he would not be able to tell the North Star from Venus.

Even the sun was a cheat. It seemed to race halfway up the sky and hang there forever. If the end of the day came as fast, they'd be out of light in no time, so after three short portages into Burke Lake and North Bay, Silas decided they would make camp on an island the map called Cigar I. On paper, it looked like the size of a football field, but it turned out to be only half as large, and a tinderbox at that. Dead pines and maples lay crossed in the fashion of a giant pyre, where shoots of dry grass filled the space between rotting trunks. With so much wind, a campfire would be out of the question, and there was hardly a spot that wasn't jagged rock on which to pitch a tent.

Neither Silas nor Meagan wore a watch. But that had been the plan. They would submit to Quetico time: sleep when they were tired, eat when they were hungry, and otherwise they would paddle. Silas tried not to dwell on how long they spent sitting on the shore, watching lucent water lick the stones beneath their feet and waiting for day to end.

"I doubt we went ten miles," Meagan said, cinching up her capris to put her calves deeper in.

"I think you're right." He checked their location on the map relative to Prairie Por, consulted the legend, and did some conversion math before gazing back across the choppy, gray water. For six hours' work paddling into the wind they had gone less than eight miles.

By the time the sun bent toward the horizon, camp was struck, the Coleman lit, the water boiled, the dinner eaten, the water boiled again, the dishes cleaned and stacked, and all with an enormity of daylight left. The night would bring some novelty, Silas hoped, and a break from the heat. As the sky darkened, he could still feel his face blister from so many hours in the sun. He recognized they should have made the island a stop for lunch rather than the campsite.

"Paddle out?" he said while there was still the thinnest film of light left.

As if she might be after something to read, Meagan put on her glasses. "Is that smart?" she said. "I mean, how good are you with that thing?" She was referring to the map. "One rock looks like every other. And in the dark?"

"To be honest, I'm more worried about the wind than getting lost."

"Let me see it," she said.

Silas slowly passed the map above the barren fire pit. He had every reservation about letting Meagan see it. At worst, she would discover they had made camp on one of the smaller islands—one that would make the real Cigar I look like a Four Seasons; if nothing else, she was bound to ask him questions about cartography he couldn't answer.

A moment later Dollar came vaulting from the darkness of the fallen trees, as happy as if he had discovered all Quetico to be his new backyard. In the space of a few minutes it became too cold, too dark, and too windy to consider going on the water. A lightning field shuttered in the distant west. Even with her glasses, Meagan appeared to have a hard time reading the map, which she seemed to regard as something more beautiful than practical.

"I don't know," she said, hesitating, then finding their location relative to the top of the fold. "Maybe we didn't do so badly. Already in North Lake? We are going north, right?"

The dog ambled up to Silas, licked his master's heel and rolled over. Silas opened their food pack and emptied a pre-measured bag of kibble onto a tin plate. A crescent moon hung low and stars were out in force, like a vast scattering of sands spread across the vault of space.

Suddenly, Meagan was hopping mad. Silas could tell by the way she held her glasses in one hand, halfway between her chin and the ground. In the other hand she held the map, removed from its sheath and unfurled above her knees like a rigid quilt. In the absence of much light at all, it looked like a lunatic had flung brushfuls of green and blue paint across a canvas.

"Are you crazy?" she murmured. "Are you fucking-out-of-your-mind crazy?"

She tapped their location on the map with her glasses. With her right index finger, Meagan pointed to Backs Bay and the outfitter's camp all the way at the top—so far north it wasn't even in Quetico, miles away and only visible when the chart was fully unfolded, exposing the enormity of the park for what it was.

Day Two, Monday

Canoes are marriage-savers. Silas had read this. Put a couple in one and sooner or later they're bound to talk. The implication is that such therapy always ends well, but as they set out he wondered if, like the divorce rate, fifty percent of the time it doesn't end in a drowning. Besides, Silas didn't feel like talking. He had not drunk enough water the day before and woke up with a headache.

By the time they arrived at the first crossing, Meagan had exhausted several tactics—anger, shame, negotiation, pleading—and had informed Silas that, unless he agreed to turn back, he would be carrying the canoe by himself and both packs across every portage.

"No problem," he said from the bow. Looking over his shoulder, Silas saw she was refusing to paddle. "We're not going back. There is no back." They had all the time in the world, he knew, now that he could properly judge the sun.

But by the second portage, at nearly a thousand meters, patience frayed. Balanced on his shoulders, the sixty-three-pound canoe swayed forward and back, grinding into his neck as he negotiated stones, root systems, and mud along the narrow path. Meagan was with the dog, somewhere behind.

Light flickered through a low canopy of jack pine and spruce. Silas let his mind wander, to think of anything other than a pressure like spring clamps pinching the back of his neck. If he were in the city, he would be following a routine and, depending on the time, either taking client calls or attending meetings. Meagan would be at home or at Zuckór, the gourmet bakery where she was a concept confectioner. Her title was only slightly more ridiculous than the work itself, which was to invent new and evermore elaborate designs for wedding cakes. It amazed Silas that it didn't amaze Meagan that, even during a recession, brides-to-be would commission designs of enormous complexity and expense (not that they were the ones paying) in a perpetual game of one-upmanship. The day before they left for Canada, Meagan had sold a design that the bakery, owing to the laws of physics, was not sure it could produce. The cost would be nearly five thousand dollars.

"For a cake?" he had said.

"Not a cake. A wedding cake."

Silas wanted to ask if it was a cake people don't consume. An interest-bearing cake, perhaps. He couldn't be expected to believe it was something to be paid for, eaten, and then shat back out. It was then, as the weight from the canoe buckled his knees and caused his muscles to twitch, Silas realized how he and Meagan were in the same business. They both relied on people willing to wager large sums of money, whether tactically or emotionally, on uncertain futures.

With each new swell of ground, Silas prayed that at the top he would see the next lake or anything at all to signal an end to the portage. It was not the time, he knew, to dwell on the fact that each step forward was the accrual of two additional steps—a return trip for the packs and then north again.

If Dollar were back in Saint Louis, Silas thought, he'd be curled up on the hardwood, probably near the window, stricken with ennui and waiting for someone to come home. If the trip was a no-lose proposition for any of them, it was Dollar. Meagan could take a lesson. She adored their pet, and it would not have surprised Silas to know she loved the dog as much as she loved him.

The nearer Silas got to the water, the thinner were the trees, until he was stumbling in quarter steps down an embankment and turning the canoe from above his head onto the surface of the water. The drop-off was immediate. The lake went from shallow for the first few meters to what was, likely, a considerable depth. He could tell the point by the color of the water at its surface, where it changed from green to black. He was beginning to learn these things, and suddenly he didn't feel quite so tired. Silas secured the painter rope to a log and sprang back up the hill, as determined as ever that Meagan should get more from the trip than she knew she had coming.

When he returned to the other side, the dog was there but not Meagan. Silas hoisted the packs, one each over his front and back, and was setting out again when she broke through a web-work of dead branches, eyes downcast and fending off stems with both arms. In Meagan's left hand was what little remained of a roll of toilet paper, several sheets from which trailed behind like a white flag of surrender.

"That's the plan, is it?" she said. "Take the dog and leave?"

"You weren't here," Silas said. "And there's a trail. Or do you expect me to carry you, too?"

"A girl needs to pee." She stood in a patch of juniper, offshoots of stick and moss clinging to her hair. Meagan would not have agreed—and it was a good thing she had not brought a mirror—but Silas thought she was more beautiful without the varnish of cosmetics.

"Better save some of that," he said, already on the move. "You'll have to do more than pee before we're done out here." Silas had not gone far before he figured out what Meagan was up to with the toilet paper. She meant to exhaust their resources so there would be no choice but to turn back. As Dollar bolted past, Silas wondered that she wasn't capable of any greater badness.

They crossed Shade Lake, then Noon, then Summer, then Silence, pushing northeast and aiming for Agnes, a tall blue swath that bridged the lower quadrant of the map to its middle and which, on the page, looked like a human spine. On arriving, it appeared more like a sea—so far across they might as well have been standing on the shore of Lake Superior. And it was getting late.

"There are islands up and down the middle," Silas said, leaning on a boulder. "Should we make for one or camp here?"

"Does it matter?"

"Forward motion," Silas said. "It matters." He had been downing water, emptying the Nalgene nearly as quickly as he could fill it from the center of lakes.

"Do you know which way is north?" Meagan said. "It looks like the ocean."

"Left," Silas said. "Left is north." He turned the tips of his fingers into the sides of his head, then consulted the map. He wanted to point out something positive, like how they had been traveling parallel to Agnes and were joining it near the halfway point, but reconsidered when he saw how far it was to the first island. "Never mind," he said. "We'll camp here."

"Is this even a site?" she said. "I don't see a fire pit."

"We'll make it a one."

"On second thought," Meagan said, "I would feel better if we camped on an island." Silas looked at her. "If there are no more portages. I'm not trying to be difficult," she said. "I'll help carry the packs if there are."

"There aren't. Not today."

"Then can we paddle to the first island?"

"What's the difference?" Silas said, his stomach quaking. "Oh, God—"

"What's the matter?"

"Nothing. Why do you care?"

"Forward motion," she said.

Silas leaned over the boulder and water leapt from his belly, running through his mouth, nose, and eyes. "Oh, God—" he gasped.

"Are you OK?"

"No. I'm not OK," he said before the next wave hit.

"Bears," she said.

"What?" Silas raised his head from behind the rock. His eyes were shot-through and red, and his chin, before he wiped it, glistened. "You know bears can swim, right?"

"If we could row to that island just out there," Meagan said, "I'd worry less." She said "just out there" like she knew where it was. It would be at least a mile, as far as Silas could tell, climbing into the canoe.

The water took on a menacing, pearl hue. The trees, while they could still see them, were already reddish-black.

The island they settled on was unnamed, as were all those in Agnes.

"I feel better about this," Meagan said when they ran aground.

Silas dragged the canoe onto the shore, dropped the bow, and kept walking. In twenty feet water was again lapping at the pebbles beneath his toes. "It's not an island," he said. "It's a rock. No campsite. No trees."

"No bears," Meagan said.

"Fuck the bears," he said. "There's nothing to cut the wind."

"It's dark now, so let's make the best of it."

"We can't so much as build a fire." Silas locked his fingers behind his head and stared Meagan down. "Do you have any idea how cold it's going to get tonight?"

"Check the map, please?" Meagan said, rummaging through the food pack for her box of graham crackers. "I'd feel better if I knew where we are."

"None of these islands have names, and they certainly don't name the rocks."

"We'll name it, then. *Isola di Tristezza*. We'll pretend we're exiles," she said, "guilty of great crimes and doomed to spend the rest of our lives here together."

"That's your idea of spending the rest of our lives together—doomed?" Dollar had already made a complete investigation of the place, two times around before seeming satisfied there was nothing more to it. Silas sat with his arms hanging over both legs. His head, still throbbing, was sunk between his knees. "Do you have any idea," he said again, "any idea at all how cold it's going to get tonight?"

Day Three, Tuesday

Without a jackhammer, there's no way to stake a tent to solid rock, but until the two confronted the bleakness of their situation, there remained some hope, at least, for a good night's rest. They used several of the larger stones to keep their gear from blowing into the lake and then huddled in a single sleeping bag, the Lab at their feet, waiting for a dawn that seemed indefinitely postponed. Only the dog slept.

When the sun reappeared, it did so with the same faint indifference by which it had vanished the night before. With no tents to fold or pack, they loaded the canoe and were back on the water early.

"You can't possibly know which way we're going," Meagan said. "Even if we were heading back, I don't see how you'd know." A widespread layer of fog hovered above the water's surface, and through it visibility was less than a few yards in any direction. It was possible to see well enough below the fog, however, as if paddling through a low tunnel. Silas navigated with his head lowered—first to one side then the other, occasionally checking over his shoulder to monitor Dollar, curled between the provisions.

"There is no back," he said, as much to break the silence as confirm his resolve. As the fog burned off, there were other things he could have said, like how, in the distance, the trees looked like a design from one of Meagan's wedding cakes. Silas thought it would have been clever, but at the same time he knew she would think he was pandering.

"Shameless," she muttered. And then there was the sound of his paddle alone pushing back the water.

"If I say we're going home, will you at least paddle?" When he looked back, Meagan's oar rested on her knees, her small hands gripping the shaft.

"You can't possibly know which way we're going," she said again. "You haven't checked the map once. You just keep looking at the damn dog."

"Leave Dollar out of this," Silas said. "We're somewhere in Agnes. Same as yesterday. Headed north."

"Somewhere . . . *somewhere.*"

"It's a big lake, Meagan. You underestimate the scale of things."

"Somewhere."

"Leave Dollar out of this," he said again. "When the fog clears, I'll show you where we are on the map."

"Somewhere."

"Yes, so will you please paddle?"

Two hours passed. Then a third. The fog cleared, and there was nothing to hide behind. No excuse not to identify their location. Under the guise of a break, Silas stopped rowing and turned the map in circles on his knees. He held out his hands to the sun—right hand in the direction it had risen, east—left along its projected path, west, meaning that north had to be straight ahead.

"What are you doing?" Meagan asked.

"Yoga. What do you think I'm doing?"

Ahead of them was a landscape of white pines, the west side of the lake, Silas thought, or the shore of a large island. He consulted the map, which shook in his hands. There were no islands in Agnes this big. They should keep going right, he determined, into the wind.

"Did it occur to you to bring the GPS?"

"We're fine. I know north from south." Silas thought he had answered too quickly to be believed, but fast enough to skirt the question or further inquiry—to keep Meagan from discovering, as well, that it had not occurred to him even to bring a compass.

Knowing the longer they put it off the more satisfying it would be, Silas suggested they not eat right away. By afternoon, the lake narrowed in a way that appeared to accord with the map, but even if they were where Silas wanted them to be, he was too exhausted from self-doubt and second-guessing for there to be much joy in it.

"There's a portage ahead," he said. Dollar lifted his head, as if he knew the word or recognized where they were. To win back some confidence, it was worth it for Silas to wager whatever credibility remained by calling out the crossing in advance. Soon, they ran aground.

"If we had brought the guide," Meagan said, collapsing onto the grass. "I mean, honest to God, at least we could have enjoyed ourselves. Yes, it still would have been hard work, but without the angst." It sounded like she was trying to talk herself into a better frame of mind, and Silas was determined not to interfere, even as he looked around with a fresh sense of distress.

"I need to sit," he said. Dollar ran around the boulders like they were old friends. The path between trees seemed familiar—similar, if not exact, in detail to the portage they had exited two days before.

"Are you all right?" Meagan asked.

Silas watched her, surrounded by grass and nightshade, its purple flowers, like conical caps, dotted with bulbs of red snake berry. *Don't say anything*, he heard a voice say. *Don't say anything*. He felt nauseous, like he had before becoming sick from dehydration.

171

"I wouldn't mind sleeping on the mainland tonight," Meagan said. "I think it would be exciting to see a bear. Do you think there are bears out here, Silas?"

Don't say anything. If she discovers the mistake, you can deal with it then, the voice said. *If not, you'll have time on the portage to find a way to explain.*

Silas got to his feet, sipped water, and called Dollar, who trotted up with several long, green stems protruding like whiskers from both sides of his mouth.

Soon after they set out, however, there was a reason to be hopeful. The landscape was less familiar and, as the map confirmed, the crossing was longer than the one from two days earlier. If they were where Silas guessed, there would be a short paddle on the far side to a longer crossing, 400 meters, ending in Keewatin Lake, and then a slightly longer portage at 420 meters.

Both expectations met with success.

As the shadows grew long, Silas was certain he knew their location. It would be a straight shot north, across the next fold in the map. Relief overcame discomfort, nagging only insofar as Silas couldn't brag about how found they were without admitting to how lost he'd thought they'd been.

"Make camp on Rose or Kasie?" he asked.

"Are those islands?"

"Yes," Silas said.

"It doesn't have to be an island," Meagan said. "I'm not afraid."

"I never said you were." Silas's breathing was labored. They had traveled twice as far in one day as in both of the previous two. "We'll camp on the west shore then," he said, "across from Rose. But we'd better find a place while there's still light."

"Are there moose?"

"Moose, bears, deer, squirrels, snakes."

"Snakes?" Meagan said.

"Whatever you're in the mood for."

"I'm never in the mood for snakes."

"There's a spot," Silas said.

Ahead of them, a crag arched thirty feet straight up from the lake before gradually descending along a slope to a cove where the water eddied in a shallow basin. The sun had sunk behind the trees at the top of the cliff, leaving the couple in the cool, gray shadows of dusk.

Things were going so well that, except for how tired he was, Silas felt it would be the perfect night to propose: a warm campsite at their back, legs dangling over the precipice, stars above. When they arrived near the shore, Silas stepped blindly into knee-deep water, carpeted at its surface with arrowhead root and foam. He offered her his hand.

"You would pick a place like this," Meagan said.

"What do you mean?"

"No sir, thank you," she said. "If I were a snake, this is *exactly* where I'd make camp."

Day Four, Wednesday

Their luck was good: a level campsite, no rain, and a night not so awfully cold. Meagan claimed to be too wary to join Silas and Dollar at the edge of the cliff, a refusal that seemed in-step with her overall aversion to adventure. So Silas lay blanketed and alone, ogling an epic view of stars and satellites. It was late when he joined her in the tent, and they slept until after sunrise.

"What day is it?" Meagan asked.

"Day four."

"What day of the week?" she said.

"Thursday?" he said. "I don't know." They sat on opposing logs, facing a ring of white ash from the previous night's fire.

"I thought it was Thursday, too," she said. "But that makes it day five."

"How so?"

"We left on a Sunday," Meagan said.

"Right. OK, so it's Wednesday."

"For the one in charge of navigation, you seem pretty cavalier about not knowing what day it is."

Fuck you, Silas thought. Leave it to her to fail to see the miracles all around them. The notion of hours, days, and weeks had never mattered less to him. She was counting down to the end, he supposed—down to how soon she could escape the raw beauty of Quetico and return to her towers of comfort and sense.

Without taking so much as a pack, Silas sprinted down to the canoe then back to the campsite, clutching a bouquet of flaccid, wet shoots. Dollar ambled up the hill behind him.

"Arrowhead," he said.

Meagan was extracting her cherished box of graham crackers from their provisions. "I hope you don't think—"

"They're edible. They taste like carrots." Silas lowered half of the crop to Dollar's mouth, and the dog devoured them without hesitation. "Here," he said, offering her some.

"Not for a million dollars," she said. "You don't even have a field guide!"

"Can you give it a rest, Meagan?" Silas said. "You wouldn't take a chance if your life depended on it. There's more to ritual than just your wedding cakes. I mean, I can understand you not tasting the pork. But this is right up your alley." He snatched the box of crackers from her and kicked the pack onto its side, out of which he grabbed the only other box of grahams, still unopened. He marched to the edge of the cliff.

174

"What are you doing?"

"You don't carry shit," he said.

Meagan caught up to him as Dollar, cued to the excitement, began running in circles.

"You don't paddle," he said. "You won't come near the cliff." As if reminded of the fact, Meagan halted two yards from the edge.

"You wouldn't," she said.

Silas was holding both boxes over the drop before he saw the silliness in it. "All I want is for you to take some chances," he said, setting the grahams at his feet and returning past her toward the campsite. "A few risks. Let's just pack up and go."

But Meagan had other plans. She stormed forward and let go with a kick that sent both boxes hurtling down to the water. She turned, arms crossed and standing defiantly at the cliff's edge. Silas gawked back.

"And so you know," she said pointedly, "I tasted the pork."

By the time Silas sculled to the base of the cliff, both cardboard boxes had floated away or sunk—not the offering he had had in mind for the spirits of the lake. Dollar, who couldn't get enough of splashing around, remained in the water until Silas re-moored the canoe, loaded it, and the three were off again.

They crossed a punishing five-hundred-meter portage connecting Kawnipi Lake to Montgomery. The sky was sapphire bright, and for the first time since they had set out, there was no wind to oppose them.

Soon, the voice returned. *Get it out*, Silas heard it say. *Get it all out into the open.*

After the crossing, over which Meagan carried her share of provisions, Silas was thinking aloud. "Left," he said. "Left is west, so left." As promising as it seemed from their location on the water, further progress north or east, according to the map, led to the crown on a thinning Medusa's head of fine lines: creeks at best, at worst arroyos splintering away from the shield and ending in remote wilderness. No portage. No path. No open water.

To find their way they would need to travel west and slightly south, across two short causeways before angling up a narrow channel to Alice Lake and north to the two longest portages in the park, *Por Bonhomme* at 1,465 meters and *Sauvage* at 2,000.

Seventy-two hours in the bush had etched away the façade of grace from both of them. Only the dog looked as he had at the start of the trip. The growth along Silas's jaw had gone from coarse to shag, and Meagan's face looked like an amphora, her red-brown cheeks peeling from exposure. Hours dragged by. They forced themselves to drink water while the dog drank at will from his bowl. In the canoe, they nibbled on rice cakes and wedges of soy cheese.

At the northern tip of Alice Lake, the entrance to the portage was uncharacteristically obvious, open and wide like the mouth of a dragon. Dark-purple boulders and other formations of wet, jagged rock rutted the shore. A wide path seemed to invite them up. Silas only needed to imagine twin fire pits as eyes atop the hill for the apparition to be complete. It would have suited him if they had had to search for the portage. If they pushed ahead, there would be enough daylight to clear *Bonhomme* and pitch camp on one of the small islands on the other side.

"What's the holdup?" Meagan said. She leapt from the canoe into shin-deep water and grabbed a pack.

"Looks like rain." Silas eyed broad strokes of stratus clouds spread across the horizon, their bottoms burning pink in the western sky.

Get it out, the voice said. *Get it all out into the open.*

176

"I won't lie," he said. "This one's almost fifteen hundred meters. I doubt I have it in me." He was already scanning the hill for evidence of a clearing or anyplace they might make camp.

"We don't have to go all the way," Meagan said.

Get it out, the voice said.

"So, what did you mean, exactly, when you said you tasted the pork?"

Meagan either didn't hear or pretended she didn't. She hoisted the second pack and turned away. Knee-deep in a tangle of grass, she seemed more confident than at any point since arriving in Quetico, and Silas wondered if her strength was fed by his weakness.

"There's a spot," she said. "Up there."

They hiked up and camped in the eye of the beast. For the first time, Silas realized the sum of all discomforts converging on him. On top of this were the fresh annoyances of blackflies and mosquitoes.

By dusk, the canopy had a hue like rusted foil. Dark red and bronze leaves tingled in the wind. Soon the sky was black. In less than an hour the world had taken on the deciduous qualities of gloom, when late summer suddenly becomes like late autumn.

"I think it would be best if we had it out," Silas said, buying Dollar to his side with a nugget of food. "About Cody," he said. "This can't go on—the trip, I mean, the way I'd planned it, until we do."

"I disagree."

"Disagree that we should have it out or that we can't go on?"

"Both," Meagan said. "Although I'm not sure what you're talking about."

Silas pondered the long-term implications of marriage vows—*as long as ye both shall live*. Licking at the space above the pit, yellow flames split sticks of maple and oak, launching sparks into the cold air.

"It's not a game." Silas leaned nearer to the fire. "I'm not playing games."

"Are you for real?" she said. "Lighten up. We're in the middle of all creation. For the first time, I'm beginning to think we can do this. Now *you're* the one going off the deep end?"

"You fucked him, didn't you?" Silas's gaze remained fixed—not on Meagan but on the fire. "When my back was turned. That's exactly what you did."

"Are you completely crazy?"

"It's okay—well, not okay—but better if you own up before it's too late."

"And just when might I have done this?" she said. "And what do you mean before it's too late? Before we die out here after you get us good and lost?"

"You'd have found a way," he said. "You're resourceful."

"If this is you trying to be helpful, it's not working," Meagan said. "What's the point, anyway? I mean, what are we talking about?"

"Everything," Silas said. "Everything's the point. I need to know. I have to know, and you still haven't said you didn't." A gust of wind bolted in from the west, twisting the flames into thin, white threads. Trees moaned and cracked from the vaults of blackness behind them.

"This is not the time," Meagan said, softening her tone and moving close enough that only Dollar separated them.

"If not now, when?"

Silas's eyes were deep, and wet, and stung with smoke. Meagan comforted him with the same absent affection by which he pacified the dog. Then, seeming lost for more to say, she suggested they turn in early before it started to rain.

178

Day Five, Thursday

Rain buffeted the tent for most of the night, and wind yowled off the lake. The downpour continued into morning, and by the time the couple was on the move, there was still little light to see by. Only the path vanishing into an iron haze was visible.

Por Bonhomme was uphill for the first thousand meters, but harder the rest of the way—a downhill slope, at a steeper grade, and with hardly any roots or low branches to grab. They fell often enough that soon every inch of exposed flesh was muddied or cut, until it seemed to Silas that there were no new injuries left. It took two trips over three hours and all that remained of the morning to cross. By then even the dog was spent.

"We should have put on raingear," Meagan said.

"It's all raingear now," Silas said. "We just need to keep the food dry."

"What lake is this?" she asked.

"No name," Silas said, flipping the chart. The most recent crossing bridged the map's previous quadrant to its top. For the first time, Silas could see both their position and base camp without opening a fold. "It's the first of two lakes before a portage that'll make the last one look like nothing."

"When did they say they'd rescue us?"

"Who?" Meagan was too tired, Silas guessed, to know how unwise it was to bring up the guides, yet aware enough not to mention Cody by name. "The guides? Two days yet," he said. "But we'll make it. Unless we get as far as the big lake, there won't be anything to rescue. If we can cross *Sauvage* today, we'll have a good chance at making Pickerel tomorrow."

"Pickerel?"

"The big lake."

"In time to be saved?"

"Nobody's saving anybody," Silas said. "The only ones here for us are us."

It took less than an hour to cross the first small lake. Under alternating spells of mist and rain, they pushed their way over slicks of still, black water, passing islands no bigger than mailboxes.

"Can we forget the past?" Meagan asked.

"What past?"

"There's that sense of humor," she said.

"No," Silas said, "I mean what part of your past do you want me to forget?"

Rather than hoist it, Silas and Meagan carried the canoe like it was a casket, over a short land bridge to the next small lake where the opposite shore was somewhat visible through the fog.

"It's late," Meagan said.

"It can't be one o'clock yet," Silas said. "It's the storm. There's lots of day left."

"What's that smell?" she said as they arrived at the shoreline. "Has something died?"

"Maybe, but sometimes vegetation can smell like that." Silas reloaded the canoe. "This'll be a quick crossing, but the portage on the other side is brutal. You up for it? We'll be practically home free after that."

"How long did you say it was?" she asked.

"Long enough," he said.

"I'm in," she said. "Forward motion."

They crossed the water and undertook *Sauvage* in silence, conserving energy to make the portage in a single pass since there would be neither the daylight nor the strength for two trips. After several hundred meters, the path opened to an overgrown field, an acre of weeds and wildflowers woven in among brambles.

Silas and Meagan flipped the canoe onto the ground and let the packs slide from their shoulders. The sun broke through, falling on clusters of berries that sparkled like rubies.

"Can we eat these?" Meagan asked, but Silas was already picking some.

"I don't know. I'll check my field guide," he said, moving a fistful into his mouth. "Amazing. Unreal." Meagan took some of the wild strawberries from him and began to eat. Silas wondered about bears, which might be drawn to such a place.

They stayed longer than he planned before discovering that there had, in fact, been bears nearby. Leaving the field, they overstepped misshapen pyramids of dung and places where the weeds were flattened.

"I wish I could say we're halfway across," Silas said, when they were back on the trail.

"It's fine," Meagan said. "Like you said, the only ones here for us are us."

They lurched ahead with the canoe on their shoulders, pressing north along a path so overgrown that at points it disappeared for meters at a time.

"Silas," Meagan said.

"Yes?" he answered from the lead.

"Nothing."

He was too exhausted to coax, reckoning Meagan had caught herself on the verge of a petty complaint.

"Silas," she said again, a few minutes later.

"What?"

"Dollar," she said. "Is he with you?"

"What do you mean?"

He turned as far as the burden of the canoe would allow, then let the Alumacraft roll from his shoulders and collide with a bank of trees on the right.

"Dollar!" Silas called. Nothing. "Not good. Dol-lar!" Silas squeezed by the canoe, unfastened his pack, and bolted back down the trail. "Dollar!"

"How far have we come?" Meagan shouted.

"How should I know? Two-thirds of the way? Maybe less?" A few minutes earlier he would have paid to see the end of *Sauvage*, but now Silas was forced to consider the implications of backtracking—how long it would take and with little daylight left. "Dollar! He always comes when we call. This isn't happening," he said. "I'm going back."

"*You're* going back?"

"We're going back. Leave the canoe. We can take the packs and make camp in the meadow." Silas wondered if Meagan was thinking the same thing. "Bears or not. We're not taking one more step without the dog," he said.

"Can we camp here?" Meagan asked.

"We're not doing anything until we find him. Besides, there's not enough room to turn the canoe, let alone pitch a tent."

"All right," she said. "All right."

"Dol-lar!"

Five minutes into the retreat, Silas spotted the dog. He must have heard his name but was still only roving down the path. Silas was so relieved he nearly crushed the animal. "We never should have brought you. Too much," he said. "Too much." He brought out a cup from his pack then offered water to the dog until he had had his fill.

When Dollar was finished, Silas hoisted his pack like it weighed nothing. "We can still make Fern Lake," he said, setting the pace north again.

"Silas," Meagan said, "I love you."

"I love you too," he said.

By the time they collected the canoe and resumed their trek, shadows were closing in from the woods and all points west. Forty minutes on, and nearly reduced to dragging the Alumacraft, they crossed a rivulet that was marked on the map and that anticipated the end of the portage by less than two hundred meters.

"It can't be long now," Silas said. "We'll camp on the shore."

When the end came, darkness had overtaken them. The lake appeared as a shroud, casting back shavings of moonlight across its surface. They were too tired to eat. Too tired to feel the cold. And so Silas and Meagan and Dollar curled up between two trees, beneath blankets, never more keenly aware of what a reward it is to sleep.

Day Six, Friday

It was late morning when they woke.

"Fern Lake's easy," Silas said. "Twenty minutes. There'll be rapids, then a short hike to Bud Lake, then Beg, then across the dam to Pickerel."

"Rapids?"

"According to the map," he said. "'Raps' near Oldfather Cove."

"You make it sound easy," Meagan said.

"I never said anything about easy."

"I said you make it *sound* easy."

They paddled to the left of an island in the middle of Fern, where the lake narrowed into a choppy run of water near a point bar and a shallow pool at the foot of the rapids. The flow was audible first, then led to a disappointing sight by Quetico standards: a forced trickle babbling down a five percent grade.

"These are the rapids?" Meagan said. "It looks like a negative class two. Should we walk the canoe up them?"

"We'll go to the side," Silas said. "The last thing we need is a sprained ankle."

They landed the canoe on a saucer of limestone and advanced alongside the water and through grass to the base of the falls, where Bud Lake emptied into Fern.

"That's more like it," he said, allowing a moment to be impressed by the surge of water thundering over the shelf. The nearer they got to active water, the more notched was the route, where the stone split into cracks as wide as a meter across.

They crossed a stretch of calm water and continued upstream to a portage connecting to Bud Lake. The day was fair. The sun was out, warm but not abusive and a welcome relief from the cold of the previous night.

"Silas," Meagan said, "I don't want to jinx us, but we're almost home free." Silas remained silent. When they stopped for lunch, he plotted how he would transfer the ring from the pouch he had sewn into the bottom of their food pack and into his jacket pocket. "Yes?" Meagan insisted. "What do you say? Almost home free?"

"Almost," he said.

Bud Lake and Beg connected along a straight, at the other side of which the couple stopped to eat before following a similar watercourse east. They soon came to a spot where they saw Pickerel pouring over a five-meter dam into a lake called Bisk. The dam's construction was simple and the first evidence either of them had seen in nearly a week that they weren't the only people on Earth. Waves splayed over four consecutive bulkheads, sending up sheets of mist and emptying Quetico's largest lake by mere drops relative to the volume of water behind. The sky faded, and where they arrived at the toe of the dam the air gathered into a crystal fog forged by kilos of water buffeting down the channel. The sound was like a jet engine.

"It's getting late," Silas yelled above the roar. "We should cross and make camp."

They reeled up the embankment to the top of the dam and then, before crossing, set the canoe off to one side. Ahead was a platform three meters wide and twenty across. There was a provisional railing lakeside, but none whatsoever above the crest gates. At all points north, the view expanded to an endless scheme of dark-blue water.

Across the top of the dam, concrete slabs alternated with metal grates, through which they could see the water siphoned from the lake to their left and racing under their feet before tumbling over the spillways to their right. Halfway across, Silas and Meagan set down their packs to rest and take in the view.

"I see a spot where we can make camp." Silas pointed to an abrasion in the landscape, a clearing of cedar that overlooked the dam north and east. "Up there."

"So close," Meagan said. "Couldn't we go farther?"

"I doubt it matters," he said. "Pickerel's all open water, and it's going to take a full day whether the wind's with us or not." They would return to the dam at night, Silas imagined, but without the dog. They would stand in this same spot, beneath an imposing moon and the unfiltered arch of stars. He would bring out the ring, fall to one knee, and say—

"Silas," Meagan said, "it's all right if you want to camp nearby. But there's something you should know."

"What?"

"The thing about Cody," she said. "You need to know. Well, because I think you already do. You were right."

Silas's weight shifted. He couldn't look at her, nor could he pretend he hadn't heard above the roar of the falls. He found himself absently examining their future campsite on the far side of the dam.

"I thought you should know," she said. "And to know that I'm sorry."

For several moments, Silas understood nothing other than the drive to go on—to forget about the campsite and the rest of the journey and the rest of their lives together and to push through what remained of Quetico, even if all at once. He turned south, in the direction they had come, taking in as much as he could of the immensity of the place and understanding how unwilling he was to confront the new and uncharted challenges of a marriage.

"I want you to know I'm sorry," Meagan said.

With strength Slias didn't know he had, he sent both packs hurtling over the crest and down the spillway. Swallowed in a crush of water and rock, they were driven to the bottom of the ravine to resurface somewhere downriver—whether at the mouth of a portage, or along the shore of Oldfather Cove, or at the head of the rapids, Silas neither knew nor cared.

Day Seven, Saturday

T-Joe and his mother, Michelle, who with her brother, Edwin, ran the outfitter, spotted them first. Not that they were lost, even if Silas had overshot the final portage—the one leading out of Quetico—by a few hundred meters.

"You would have caught it soon enough," Michelle said, searching for a way to soothe an anguish she could only guess at.

186

"I'm impressed. You guys must have flown that canoe up here if you were only at Bud Lake last night."

It was several hours after dark when they arrived at base camp, and later still before the two had showered and were sitting at opposite ends of a stone hearth. Michelle, T-Joe, the grandmother, and Edwin presided over a small ceremony initiating the *mangeurs de lard* into the society of *voyageurs*—a baptism, of sorts, by water and strong cider. The other guides, including Cody, had left Backs Bay for the season and were already at their respective universities for the fall term.

The grandmother drank a Maudite, while the rest had coffee as Michelle purposefully stoked the fire. She talked about closing up for winter and their plans for the year ahead. All the while, Meagan thumbed at a diamond on the third finger of her left hand.

"I'll be getting married next year," she reported, as distant as an oracle. "Silas proposed." She stopped fidgeting long enough for the ring to be seen, but without actually showing it off. "Last night," she said, anticipating the question. "While we were still in the canoe. He asked, and I said yes."

"I'm sorry about the equipment," Silas jumped in. "We'll cover the cost, of course." He seemed to be drifting between two places in time, surfacing intermittently. He only admitted that they had lost both packs, and with them the supplies, over the side of the dam. The hows and whys Silas could not have explained if he had had to and so was glad no one asked.

Nor did anyone ask about the dog, which was the greatest blessing. Not asked, he realized, because no one knew to. Except for Cody, who would have known he'd be gone by the time they got back, nobody realized it had not just been the two of them.

"Congratulations!" Michelle said, too enthusiastically for the silence to support.

"Thank you," Meagan said.

Nobody had asked about Dollar and nobody would, Silas concluded, even if it was the one story about Quetico he could have told better than any other. They would be wed in the secret of the loss, how the pup leapt out after the second pack, the one in which his food was stowed, above the flashboards and into the whitewater below.

Silas slipped at least a dozen times, staggering onto the riprap to recover the body, which they buried at the top of the abutment. Even after a hot shower, dark resin stained his hands from the cross he had fashioned from shoots to mark the place. It was the bitterest of ceremonies and it took a while to get right, but not before he had forgiven Meagan—the one thing a person cannot do for himself, never more easily, or more urgently, given away.